G000127241

Dearest Millie

The Pennington Family Series

May McGoldrick

Thank you for reading. In the event that you appreciate this book, please consider sharing the good word(s) by leaving a review, or **connect with the authors**.

Dearest Millie (Pennington Family Series)
Copyright © 2018 by Nikoo K. and James A. McGoldrick

All rights reserved. Except for use in any review, the reproduction or utilization of this work in whole or in part in any form by any electronic, mechanical or other means, now known or hereafter invented, including xerography, photocopying and recording, or in any information storage or retrieval system, is forbidden without the written permission of the publisher: MM Books.

Edited by Christa Soulé Désir, at EditorChrista.com

Cover by Dar Albert, at WickedSmartDesigns.com

Dedication

To all who have fought the battle,
to all who continue to fight,
and to the families and friends who
support them.

Chapter 1

The Abbey
Western Aberdeen
The Scottish Highlands

Dearest Millie,

I should be working, but the golden sun is descending in the southwest, lighting my work room with a magical glow. In the gardens beneath the window, I hear my patients being brought in for their supper. I cast my gaze around at the disarray in this office and think for the thousandth time: *I should keep better order here. Millie would not approve.*

My thoughts rarely stray far from you, my love. Every memory of you is as brilliant as this setting summer sun. And like that celestial orb, my living recollection of all our time together only dips beneath the summer horizon for a few moments, it seems, before emerging again to light my day.

Star-crossed lovers! I hear the term often, but it does not apply to us. If fate had any part in our history, dearest Millie, it played a benign role in the end.

Our introduction was not an easy one, to be sure. Chance did indeed seem to be interfering. All those opportunities to meet, thwarted...

The first time you came to the Abbey, I was in Aberdeen on business. You were passing through with the intention of visiting with your sister and her new husband, my fastidious partner, Wynne Melfort. When I returned, I found my office had been completely reorganized. Books and journals were put away on shelves and in bookcases. Files were boxed and marked alphabetically by case. The floors were completely cleared, and my carpets shaken out. And my desk—there you went *too* far, m'lady—tidy and clean, pens and ink bottles lined up like soldiers on parade. And a fresh blotter! Every surface gleamed. Unheard of doings!

I must admit, I never knew the wood of my desk had such beautiful markings in the grain.

You, however, escaped my wrath, continuing your travels north by the time I returned.

After that, I longed for an opportunity to meet the much talked-about and mysteriously alluring sister-in-law of my partner, the woman who organized my office. I just missed you when I journeyed to Edinburgh that autumn to confer with old colleagues at the medical college. You were in Hertfordshire with your parents, cowardly lass that you are. Your sister Lady Phoebe happened to be at your family home on Heriot Row. I must say, she delighted in helping me to rearrange your rooms and turn every book in your personal library upside down.

I soon learned, to my mild dismay, that Pennington women are not to be trusted. You were duly informed of my efforts to disrupt your life. The following spring when I returned from only a short stay in Aberdeen—where I'd gone to engage a new doctor to assist me at the hospital here—I found you had again come and gone like a thief in the night. You can only imagine my surprise to discover the entrance to my office had been stolen. Where the door had once been, I found a row of bookcases that had formerly lined the walls of my work place. And, curiously enough, all the books were in order, by author, an organizational concept I admit I never once considered. I knew immediately the identity of my office thief.

Then, finally, my moment arrived, when I received an invitation to the Summer Ball at Baronsford. I was not about to miss this opportunity again, for you would be there. How strangely fate works, however, that we were destined to run into each other—albeit without introduction—only a few days before . . .

Chapter 2

Edinburgh, Scotland
June 1819

No tombs lined the walls of the silent, murky foyer where Millie Pennington stood numb and frozen. This was no ancient crypt with some carved effigy of a crusading knight and his lady lying on a stone slab, blankly staring for all eternity upward into the shadows of a vaulted ceiling. But when the door to the doctor's consultation room closed behind her, Millie felt sealed in, caught in an eternity of muted desolation, cut off from the world of light and air.

She turned her head at the faint sound of a funeral bell tolling somewhere in the great city. The dark walls wavered around her, moving inward, encroaching menacingly. The distant knell ceased, and her shallow breaths were again the only sound. The small fan-shaped window over the door to the street admitted a brownish light through the soot-covered glass. So far, she'd been able to hold her emotions in check, but now she felt her insides implode. Then the tears came, covering her cheeks and dripping from her chin like ice thawing and pouring from a slate roof.

Not so long ago, her life had been in perfect order, arranged just as she wished it. Twenty-six years of age, she was the youngest daughter to the Earl and Countess of Aytoun. She had four loving siblings, all married with children and another baby on the way. Millie was a creature of tidiness and efficiency, of plans, of thinking through every step she was to take for all the days and months and years ahead. Financially secure, she would be happy to marry if the right man came along, but she could also see herself growing comfortably older and caring for her aging parents. She would be the ideal, doting aunt to a generation of nieces and nephews.

How quickly one's dreams shattered! Fate had such immeasurable power! It could, in an instant, hurl one from a precipice into a bottomless abyss.

The musty smell of the foyer threatened to suffocate her. Millie couldn't breathe. She had to get out.

She pushed out the door and stumbled down the stairs. The cobbled lane was slick with the recent rain, and the smoky Edinburgh air offered little relief. The acrid stench of a thousand coal fires stung her nose and lungs, but her mind was elsewhere, filled with countless faces demanding answers.

Millie was a devoted daughter, the most agreeable of all her brothers and sisters. She was a selfless and generous friend. She'd carved out a life path paved with compassion and kindness. She'd walked upon it with a clear conscience.

Still.

She moved forward a few steps, numb and unheeding of where her feet were taking her. Blurred grey and brown brick crowded her on either side.

Why me?

Millie's knees wobbled as faintness overtook her. She staggered, falling against a wall. Leaning there, she held a handkerchief to her face and tried to force air into her lungs.

Opium, arsenic, salve, balms. Prayers. Lots and lots of prayers. At some time during the consultation today, she'd stopped hearing the suggestions.

Fresh tears sprang onto her cheeks. She couldn't tell anyone. She couldn't tell her family. Not even Phoebe. Two years apart in age, the sisters were closest in age. They were the best of friends, confidantes. But Phoebe was due to have a child next month. Millie would never ruin her sister's happiness by sharing her news. What she'd learned today must be her own cross to bear.

Millie pushed away from the wall. At the bottom of the lane sat Cowgate, and the thoroughfare was a blur of pedestrians and vendors, carts and carriages. As she moved toward it, a narrow wynd on her left led into a dismal close. Two ragged children stood wide-eyed, watching her, just inside next to a pile of refuse.

She motioned to them, and they approached warily. Emptying her purse into their hands, they stared, suspicious of such unknown generosity. The younger girl tried to give her back the bank notes.

"It's yours to share. All of it. Go. *Go*," she urged. The two ran off, disappearing into the murky close.

"I won't need it. Not today." Her voice shook, her vision clouded. "Not tomorrow. Not ever."

She was speaking to no one. They were gone.

Still looking in the direction they'd gone, Millie turned to start down the lane again and immediately bumped into a man coming briskly up from Cowgate.

Dermot McKendry was late, as usual, but the sight of a woman emptying her reticule into the outstretched hands of street urchins immediately caught his attention. His mind had been on the meeting with a former medical colleague of his, an anatomist connected with the Surgeon's Hall, not a stone's throw from here. The man kept consulting rooms in the building at the end of the lane, and he'd recently published a treatise on erratic behavior following traumatic head injuries. Dermot had founded the Abbey Hospital, a licensed private asylum for those suffering from mental disorders caused by injury or disease in the hills west of Aberdeen, specifically to treat such patients, and he was eager to hear his friend's latest observations.

The woman never saw him before they collided, and Dermot reached out to steady her. She was medium in height, young, from what he could tell. The words of apology forming on his lips were forgotten the moment his gaze fell on her distraught face. As she recovered her footing, her chin dropped to her chest, and the bonnet effectively blocked his view of the pale visage. But not before he saw the tears.

He was stunned for a moment. He knew her.

They'd never actually met, had never been introduced, but he recognized Millie Pennington from her portrait in the family's Heriot Row home in Edinburgh. He'd been fascinated by her for a year, eager for the moment when they'd finally be introduced. Her playful sense of humor engaged him, her insistence on bringing order to his life tickled him.

Dermot felt as tongue-tied as a schoolboy, and his words became jumbled as he tried to speak. "M'lady —"

"Pardon me, sir."

Without uttering another syllable, she disengaged herself and hurried down the lane. Dermot looked after her, speechless, and in less than a moment, she'd disappeared around the corner.

What was she doing here? he wondered.

She was clearly quite distressed. He recalled her words to the waifs. *I won't need it. Not today. Not tomorrow. Not ever.*

The grey eyes had been full of tears, and her demeanor reminded him of a person in mourning. Dermot immediately thought of the Pennington family and what he'd come to know about them. Lord Aytoun, her father, was advancing in age, as was her mother. But he'd heard no ill tidings about them. He would have, for he'd come south from the Highlands to attend their Summer Ball at Baronsford.

Not that he had any interest in dancing. He'd come for one reason only — to meet Millie Pennington.

He turned to go after her. By the time he reached the thoroughfare, she was gone, lost in the bustling crowds and the traffic. He'd never find her now.

Retracing his steps, Dermot picked up a card he'd seen fall onto the cobblestones when she was giving her money to the children.

Immediately, he recognized the physician's name.

Chapter 3

Baronsford. A fairy-tale castle surrounded by farms, meadows, and forest. Riding in his hired carriage along the winding road leading to the front door, Dermot passed a shimmering loch that disappeared into a green grove.

Five days had passed since he'd last seen her. Five days since he'd abused his position in the medical profession and cajoled Millie Pennington's physician into revealing the truth of why a patient matching her description — for she'd not used her real name — was so upset after consulting with him.

Dermot stared across the fields at the River Tweed, meandering past on its way to the sea. How many poets had written of life as a river, carrying one through the turbulence and trials of this frail existence? He knew sickness well. He'd seen it in its many forms—on the sea, in the surgery, in the hospital bed. He'd tended to the infirmities of strangers and those he'd loved dearly.

Tomorrow offered no promises, regardless of how healthy one appeared or how much worldly wealth one possessed. Change was the only constant, and the same end awaited all. What mattered was that life needed to be embraced. Today. This moment.

His mind slipped back through the years. Millie's tear-stained face was replaced with another. Susan's pale and sunken cheeks, and her blue eyes, filled with despair, appeared again like a wandering specter, reminding him, cautioning him about all that could go wrong. He ran a hand over his face and forced down once again the decade-old ache, hiding it from the world, keeping his pain shut up tightly in his heart.

The blur of memories cleared as his carriage approached the gated courtyard. Baronsford was alive and clearly thriving. The grandeur of the place was both inspiring and daunting.

The wealth and power of the Penningtons were legendary, as was their reputation for hospitality. The local gentry and anyone with the slightest connection to the family waited with anticipation for the two days a year when Baronsford opened its doors to outsiders. But the family was also famous for their tight-knit loyalty.

He wondered if Millie had told them. Many people in her situation often refused to share their news with loved ones. They preferred to lock their secret away. Looking at the line of carriages ahead of him, he had his doubts that she'd said anything. If the Penningtons knew of Millie's illness, this ball would not be taking place.

A few moments later, Dermot ascended the steps past footmen and other servants, and entered a magnificent foyer. He was a first-time visitor, but he didn't share any of the open enthusiasm being voiced by other guests around him. Before tall double doors leading into the huge Palladian-style ballroom, a crowd dressed in their finest gowns and evening clothes jostled for a better place as they waited to enter. The music of Haydn blended with the sounds of revelers inside.

Realizing he needed to put on a more festive demeanor before entering, he made his way to a window overlooking the courtyard. He was accustomed to presenting an amusing façade to those around him. Over the years, Dermot had mastered the art of hiding pain behind a persona of charm and humor. And in his experience, people saw only what he allowed them to see. Or what they desired to see. Few had any interest in finding out why a distinguished physician from the finest university in Scotland would suddenly choose to become a ship's surgeon for a decade and then invest his inheritance and education in the founding of an asylum.

He looked away from the other guests.

Millie. He was here for Millie.

He was a doctor, he told himself. He had a duty to help if he could. Any physical ailment was a challenge, and it was natural to feel extreme sadness and even grief after learning the truth. But he knew, better than anyone, the destructiveness of grief.

In the ballroom, the orchestra struck up a waltz. The throng of waiting guests had dwindled, and through the doors, he scanned the reception line. The family was together. The mood appeared jovial. Nothing seemed amiss.

Except that Millie was not among them.

"Dr. McKendry, you're here."

Dermot turned around and smiled at the son of his partner, Wynne Melfort. Cuffe was dressed like a duke and exuded the confidence and self-assurance of a young man well beyond his eleven years. Though he still had a lock of unruly hair draped across his brow, he was a different person since the family had returned from Jamaica, bringing Cuffe's grandmother back with them.

Cuffe gestured toward the door. "I can show you another way in, if you don't care to meet the family right off. Lord Aytoun is a gruff one on the outside, but kindly as an old parson once he knows you. The viscount is exactly the same."

Dermot knew of the men from information Jo had shared. He also knew of the duel between the viscount, Hugh Pennington, and Wynne years ago. The two stood next to each other now, exchanging friendly barbs as if nothing had ever divided them.

Dermot stared beyond the receiving line, and he could still see no sign of Millie.

"But the women folk in my family are all soft as combed wool." Cuffe's brown eyes lit up his face. "Lady Aytoun is the best, warm as summer sunlight."

He wasn't surprised to hear this. Those of her children he'd met reflected the same warmth.

Cuffe pointed to another door. "Still, if we go out the library doors, we can get in through the gardens—"

He shook his head. "Thanks, lad. I'm looking forward to meeting the family." He paused. "But I'd like to see Lady Millie first, and she doesn't appear to be in the reception line."

"I heard she's not coming down for the ball."

"Why not? Is she unwell?"

"A headache. I heard Lady Jo talking to the doctor. She's resting in her room."

No one stood between Dermot and the ballroom. It was time to go in, but instead, he glanced up the wide staircase. "Can you take me up to her?"

"What are your intentions?" Cuffe glared at him. "Even *I* know that would not be appropriate."

Dermot smiled, hearing Wynne's tone in his son's words. "I promise you, my intentions are entirely honorable. Strictly professional. You have no need to fear for her reputation."

Cuffe shook his head and brushed the lock of hair back from his forehead. He cast a quick look at the two liveried doormen flanking the entry to the ballroom. "You need to be introduced to the family first."

At any other time, Dermot might have laughed, confronted with this guardian of decorum. Cuffe was like a son to him. They saw each other every day. One day a week, he shadowed Dermot through the hospital wards. On another day, he read to the patients and answered mail for those who weren't capable of writing to their families themselves. Here at Baronsford, after Wynne and Jo, Cuffe knew Dermot better than anyone.

"I'll meet them all in good time. But if you must know, lad, I have a gift for Lady Millie."

This news was met with a look of skepticism. "But you haven't *met* her, have you?"

"Well, no," he admitted. "But as you know, we have been communicating . . . in a manner of speaking."

"And so far, she has the better of you." Cuffe puffed up proudly. "I helped her rearrange your work room the last time she visited the Abbey."

Clearly, Dermot would have to make him an accomplice. "Then you know this is my turn to strike?"

"Strike?" The lad's gaze narrowed. "So, this is not a gift, then?"

"It's a gift." He tried to sound reassuring. "It's something Lady Millie definitely can use in her life right now."

Cuffe's suspicions were hardly allayed.

"Very well," Dermot said flatly. "Admittedly, there is a wee bit of retribution involved here."

"I thought as much."

"But if it will make you feel better, let's do this—you take me to Lady Millie's door, and I'll let you personally oversee the delivery of her gift."

Millie hugged her middle and gazed vacantly out the window at the streaks of red and gold coloring the western sky. Rows and rows of carriages tended by grooms and drivers filled a newly shorn hayfield by the stables. Distant melodic strains came to her with the soft breeze, growing intermittently louder and then softer.

She imagined her parents, Hugh, and his wife, Grace, and the others were probably finished receiving their guests by now. Her father, who had nearly been killed in a fall from a bluff overlooking the river in his youth, would need to be resting his leg. Hopefully, Phoebe was already sitting. Her pregnancy had not been the most comfortable for her.

She should be down there, Millie thought, but she just couldn't face all those people.

Each of the Penningtons, young and old, was expected to attend the event. Despite the revelry and the excitement, tonight was not about the fine gowns or the impressive carriages or the rattling gossip of the ton about the family's magnificent home. At the heart of the ball was the comingling of people from vastly different social circles.

Those with worthwhile projects had the opportunity to bring attention to their charities. And the wealthy were provided with causes they could support. A venture to provide work for immigrants in Glasgow. A new school for the children of the streets in Edinburgh. Jo's project of developing shelters for women always needed expansion, in Scotland and in England. The endeavors were many, and the members of the ton in attendance knew that by the time the night was over, their generosity would be tested.

Despite the worthiness of the evening, Millie still couldn't go down. She wasn't ready to test her courage in public. Her tears had run dry before she ventured back to Baronsford, but she had so much to consider, so much to plan. If she was somewhat subdued when she arrived, her reserve caused no alarm. Her apparent tranquility was taken for granted.

The last-minute announcement that she'd decided not to go downstairs, however, had brought both her parents to her rooms. This was not the Millie they knew, and her assurance that she only needed to rest did little to alleviate their concern. Dr. Namby, always an early guest at the ball, was immediately brought up to see her. Millie had no trouble convincing the village doctor that her headache was the result of exhaustion and nothing else.

The sounds of a waltz wafted in on the scent of roses from the trellises below her window, and Millie moved back to her writing desk and picked up the book she'd been reading. Lord Byron's tragedy, *Manfred*. Drawing a folded paper from its pages, she sat, studying the image of the three-masted ship at the top of the sheet. It was a handbill she'd picked up in Edinburgh. She read it over again.

To Sail 1st August
FOR NEW YORK
The Well-Known Packet Ship
FRIENDS
Thomas Choate, Commander
400 Tons Burthen, Copper-fastened, and newly
Coppered to the Bends, (lately arrived from
Charleston in 21 days), has superior furnished
accommodations for Passengers; and a Cow on Board
to supply them with Milk.
Shippers and Passengers *are requested to have*
Goods or Luggage, intended for this Vessel, at Leith,
by Thursday the 29th, at farthest.
For Freight or Passage, apply to:
Messrs. Stevenson, Miller, & Co., Leith;
the Captain on board;
or
JOHN FYFE & CO.
Edinburgh, 11th June, 1819

Before coming down from the city, Millie wrote to Mr. Fyfe, securing passage for herself.

She would wait until after the ball to tell her family she was leaving for America. Perhaps it would be best to wait until Phoebe had her baby next month. Everyone would be far too happily distracted to object.

New York. From there, Millie would secure passage on a mail coach or a coastal packet going to Boston, where her uncle Pierce and his wife, Portia, lived. Once she'd visited with them, she'd travel through the former colonies until it was time.

Time. She thought about a line she'd read in Byron's work earlier. *Do you think existence depends on time?* Much of the physician's words during the consultation had been lost in a fog. She did recall hearing the words *six months*, but also the physician asserted there was *no way of knowing for certain.*

The knock on the door startled Millie, and she shoved the handbill inside the book and stood. She decided it must be one of the women in her family, coming on orders from their mother to check on her.

"You may enter," she called. "I'm not asleep."

A moment later, the knock came again.

Any of the servants would have already come in, and her family would have shown less hesitation. Baronsford was bustling with guests. The idea of someone accidentally ending up here was a possibility, but hardly likely. For generations, the Pennington family had been a target of rumors and often malicious gossip. Millie could only imagine the stories going around in the ballroom regarding her absence. And here she was, about to "confirm" that she'd been banished, confined in her room. Another knock.

Millie tightened the belt on her dressing gown and stole a glance at her pale reflection in the mirror. Well, she definitely looked ghastly.

Crossing the room, she opened the door just as the young man was about to rap on it again.

"Cuffe? What are you doing up here? Has something happened?" she asked, reaching out and taking his hand.

Worry raced through her, and Millie's mind immediately filled with possible disasters. She couldn't imagine the eleven-year-old leaving the festivities unless he'd been directed to bring her a message.

"Is it Phoebe? Is she in labor? Is it my father? Has someone fallen sick?"

"Nothing is wrong." The dark brown eyes flickered to a man standing silently nearby. "I'm here to supervise the delivery of a gift."

Surprised, Millie noticed the tall man. The white brocade waistcoat of satin and the starched silk cravat provided a sharp contrast to the ebony jacket encasing impressively wide shoulders. She stared at the angular lines of his face, the alert dark eyes, the short but untidy hair that showed evidence of restless fingers running through it. The touch of a smile pulled at his lips as if challenging her to guess who he was. She wracked her memory. He looked familiar, and yet she couldn't quite place when or where she'd been introduced to the gentleman.

"Lady Millie Pennington," Cuffe said formally, ending the suspense, "may I introduce Dr. Dermot McKendry."

Unexpected delight swept through her, and she smiled . . . for the first time in days. For a moment, all was well. Her world, as she knew it, was spinning smoothly on its axis, and tomorrow was another day, as joyful and full of hope as today.

"M'lady." He bowed.

She smoothed the dressing gown. Suddenly, she felt awkward about how she looked and how she was dressed. For months now, she'd imagined this introduction. Dr. McKendry fascinated her. She was enthralled by what she knew of his work, of his passion for helping the forgotten and ignored.

Of course, she'd been somewhat mischievous in setting aright the chaos of his office when she'd visited her sister. And, if she were honest with herself, Jo's description of the doctor's boyish good looks and sense of humor had only added to her interest.

She curtsied. "Dr. McKendry. At last, we meet."

"I was disappointed to find you weren't well enough to be downstairs. I wanted to offer my services."

"Thank you. My . . . infirmity came on quite unexpectedly."

"It generally does," he replied. "And how are you feeling now?"

Reality rushed back. Lies and lies and more lies would be her only answer. She touched the side of her head. "Already improving. I shall be perfectly well by tomorrow."

"Excellent. Then may I call on you in the morning? I've been eager to—"

"I apologize, but I can't. I'm traveling to Edinburgh tomorrow." She spoke the truth. She'd already decided it would be much easier to hide her situation and mourn her fate away from the family. She didn't have any desire to try and act brave amongst them. She was no stoic, and she didn't know how long her veneer of calmness would hold up.

"That's much better for me too." He sounded pleased. "I was going to make arrangements to stay at the George Inn in Melrose Village an extra night. Now I have no reason for it. I'll be going back to Edinburgh, as well, and I can call on you there."

She couldn't do this. Millie didn't want to encourage a friendship that couldn't be. She was no longer the woman who had challenged and teased him in his absence.

"Dr. McKendry, I'm afraid my schedule—"

"Perhaps," Cuffe cut in, "perhaps if you offered Lady Millie your gift, she might change her mind."

She'd totally forgotten about her nephew standing and listening to their conversation. Millie followed Cuffe's gaze and saw a basket with a hinged top sitting at the doctor's feet.

"Of course, my gift." He picked it up. "May I carry it in for you?"

She'd organized his office. He'd created havoc with her books. Their interaction might be construed by some as having extended beyond society's rules of polite engagement.

Millie was certain she heard something thump inside as he lifted it. "What's in there?"

"Let's open it and find out."

She shook her head. "You'll tell me first."

"What are you afraid of, m'lady? It's an innocent gift."

Cuffe moved away from the door as the doctor came closer, holding the basket up. Another thump.

"It's alive," she exclaimed. "There *is* something alive in that basket."

"I certainly hope so."

"But he won't be alive for much longer if you don't let him out soon," Cuffe chipped in.

She backed away. Dermot McKendry had already proved himself a capable mischief-maker. "Well, I don't know . . ."

But it was too late. The doctor followed her in, dropped to one knee, and threw open the top.

A pig. A young blue-eyed pig, slathered with grease, blinked as it looked up at her. Millie stared back in disbelief. A puppy. Perhaps a kitten. Seconds ago, she'd decided those were the only gifts the man would dare deliver in a basket to her room. But a pig?

"Dr. McKendry, why on earth would you bring a . . .?" That was all she was able to say before the porker squealed and leapt out of the basket, bolting across the floor and leaving tracks of grease across Millie's Persian carpet. "*Stop!*"

The pig, however, was already racing in circles around the room, clearly too young to understand her command.

She shrieked as the beast dashed by, nearly knocking her over and leaving a mark on her dressing gown as it glanced off her leg.

"Dr. McKendry, *stop* that animal!"

"I'm trying." He leapt into the pursuit. "Stand there, I'll steer him toward you."

She wanted to kill the man. "Not toward *me*."

"You're by the basket."

She kicked the basket away. "I'm not about to—"

The piglet ran by the fireplace, and the rack of andirons went flying, making clanging noises as the tools scattered across the hearth and the wood floor.

"You missed him!" McKendry exclaimed as the panicked creature streaked past her, grazing a candle stand.

Millie clutched for the stand as it teetered.

"You must put more effort into this," he admonished.

She forcibly restrained herself from swinging the stand at his head. "Trust me. You don't want me putting more effort in anything right now."

"Fits of temper will only rile such a wee, sensitive pet."

"My *wee, sensitive pet* won't be the recipient of any *fits of temper*." She positioned herself in the animal's path, deciding it was up to her to catch it. "But you . . . you . . ."

"I know. You don't have to say it. You are so pleased with my gift. You're at loss for words to express it."

Millie wanted to throw something at him.

"Here he comes again. Catch him," Cuffe yelled.

Millie grabbed at him, but the pig squirted through her hands, throwing its slippery body at the bed. "No!"

Too late.

She staggered as she dove for the little demon, nearly falling as her slippered foot went out from under her. The troublemaking doctor's arm was around her waist. For a moment they stood too close. Her hand pressed against his chest. Her lips were inches away from his. Her heart's beating was loud enough that she was certain he could hear it. A delicious twist knotted in her belly, and she shot a look at his face and saw laughter. She was disappointed when he set her on her feet and stepped back.

The bedspread was marked, probably forever. As were her grease-covered hands. She was satisfied to see her handprint on his satin vest.

"My books!"

Across the room, the porker hit the small pedestal table by her reading chair and squealed bloody murder as the neat stack of books showered down on its greasy body.

"I'll get him," McKendry shouted as the piglet sprinted by him and disappeared under the bed.

"Come out, you beast!" she cried out, going down on her hands and knees next to the bed.

The man's shoulder pressed against hers as he joined her on the floor. Their hips touched. "Come out, Satan!" he commanded. The man was no help.

The two of them sprawled on the floor as they both reached for the animal. Suddenly, unexpected images filled her head, and corresponding sensations, thrilling and ill-timed, pulsed through her body. His body on top of hers. Hers on top of his. Millie didn't know what he'd done to her.

"I'll never forgive you," she muttered, needing to clear her head but unwilling to edge away from him. "What on earth possessed you—?"

"I must say . . . There he goes, Cuffe!" he shouted as the pig went out the other way. "If you're not going to take better care of my gifts..."

Millie sat up on the floor, surrounded by the uproar of a squealing piglet and an excited eleven-year-old in pursuit, and all to the accompaniment of a waltz in the distance. Her clean and orderly room looked like a tempest had ripped through it. Her dismal mood was now a vague memory. She touched the greasy stains on her formerly immaculate dressing gown and decided she liked the contrast of colors. The absurdity of it all was too much, and laughter bubbled up inside her.

As the piglet passed them again, the doctor made a dive for him, and a rending sound came from his pants as a seam gave way.

"They probably heard that tear in Melrose Village," she commented, unable to resist.

He sat back against the bed, and the look on his face was priceless. She couldn't stop herself from giggling out loud, and he joined her as the pig continued to run circles around them. Millie laughed until she could barely breathe. Cuffe sank into a chair across the room.

"Perhaps since I've been wounded, I might call on you in Edinburgh the day after tomorrow. I'm sure by then you'll find a suitable way of thanking me for my gift."

Before Millie could reply, she saw the piglet's eyes dart toward the open door.

"*No!*" she shrieked.

Seeing freedom within his grasp, the little devil bolted from the room and disappeared down the hallway.

Chapter 4

Two Days Later

Millie stood at a front window in the drawing room, her book tucked under her arm, staring down at the traffic moving past on Heriot Row. Her mood demanded a grey and rainy day, but nature refused to cooperate. The morning sky over Edinburgh's New Town was azure blue and crystal clear. She pulled the window open and smelled the balmy fresh air as it wafted in. Outside, people were riding by in open carriages.

Still no sign of him, she thought. Perhaps he wasn't coming.

She'd risen early, as she usually did, and started the day telling her maid and the housekeeper and the butler and anyone else she crossed paths with that she would not be receiving any callers today.

Neighbors seemed to know when one of the Penningtons had arrived in town, for the stream of guests and invitations always began immediately. Friends and even vague acquaintances were daily callers whenever Lord or Lady Aytoun or any of their children were in Edinburgh. But Millie was hardly in the mood for entertaining or being entertained. But, she admitted to herself, it wasn't friends or acquaintances on her mind right now. It was Dermot McKendry, and she was still debating whether she should see him or not.

Tired of Lord Byron and her own dark thoughts, Millie recalled the nonsensical scene the night of the ball. Before the man arrived, she hadn't believed she would ever laugh again. He'd proved her wrong.

If he came this morning and sent up his card, Millie mused, and she didn't receive him, he would certainly see it as a rebuff. He didn't deserve that. The footmen and the butler could certainly manage a lie for her, but perhaps it would be better if she wrote to him and explained…

No. There was nothing she could say in a note that would make him understand what she was going through or what she was feeling.

Millie paced the drawing room. She didn't want to reject him. Not as a person. Not as a . . .

as a what? As a friend? Her thoughts again returned to the night of the ball. She pressed a fist against her stomach, not wanting to dwell on the physical awareness that had rushed through her. Instead, she focused on the pig. The greased pig. The mayhem didn't end in her room either. The animal made it down the stairs and into the ballroom where the roars of the guests were louder than the squeals of the terrified animal. Luckily, a footman had been able to catch it before any harm befell the little beast.

She was surprised to hear a chuckle and realize she had been the one to laugh. She shook her head, still smiling to herself.

McKendry's reprisal had indeed been a good one. The devil.

A carriage rolled to a stop in front of the house. Millie hurried to the open window, and her gaze fixed on the man stepping out onto the sidewalk, carrying what looked to be a satchel under one arm.

Her sister Jo had certainly not exaggerated Dr. McKendry's fine looks. Two nights ago, she'd been caught off her guard, but now she stared at him, appreciating the details of his face. The finely wrought cheekbones. The straight nose. The high, intelligent brow. Confidence was written in every line and in his stride as he walked toward the house. He was an enticingly handsome man, and she felt the flutter deep in her belly.

Her ogling came to a quick halt when he directed his eyes upward to the window where she stood gaping. He stopped and lifted his hat to her. Millie, overwhelmed by the heat that rushed through her, remained locked in place for a moment but then quickly backed away.

Oh, no. He'd seen her, and in a moment the butler was going to tell him she wasn't home. That wouldn't do. It wouldn't do, at all.

As the knock sounded on the front door, she hurried out and was able to cut off the footman before he opened it. She quickly gave him her instructions. Retreating to the drawing room, Millie tried to compose herself before he was shown in. What was a visit of twenty minutes or so, anyway? Their personal history demanded she give him that courtesy. He was simply calling on her to ask after her health. Nothing more than that. She took several deep breaths.

There wasn't much time to fret as a soft knock was quickly followed by the footman announcing the caller.

"Dr. McKendry, how kind of you." A curtsy and a bow were exchanged. "What are you delivering today, if I may ask?" She gestured to the satchel he had tucked under the arm. "A hive of bees? Adders, perhaps?"

"I don't know what would possess you to think I'm capable of such callousness." He surveyed the room. "But now that you mention it, what did you do with my gift?"

She arced an eyebrow. "Do you really want to know?"

"Please don't tell me he was delivered to the kitchen and used as the main course for dinner yesterday."

"Hardly. At present, I believe he's terrorizing the kennels at Baronsford, for I decided to keep him as a pet. In fact, I've already named him."

She motioned to a chair for him to sit. He shook his head. "Named him?"

"I'm calling him 'Dermot.' Don't you think that's a fine name?"

His laugh warmed her, and she smiled.

"I'd say that *is* a fine name. I hope he wears it with pride."

Millie gestured toward a chair again. "May I offer you some refreshments, Doctor?"

"I'd like to stay, but I can't." Pulling the satchel from under his arm, he opened it and began to reach inside. "I have lecture notes here that were entrusted to me by a friend of mine who teaches at the Royal College of Surgeons. I need to comment and return them today. I didn't want you to think less of me for making this such a brief visit."

Millie frowned at the thick ream of paper he was struggling to remove from the leather bag. "How could I think any less of the one person who successfully brings mayhem into my life?"

"Very kind of you . . . I think." He shifted the satchel to get a better grip on the papers.

"You don't need to show me. I believe you."

"Nay, I insist."

Clearly frustrated, he yanked the stack of paper from the satchel. An instant later, pages were flying in every direction, descending like autumn leaves.

Shocked by the suddenness of it, Millie stared as a breeze from the window compounded the chaos, riffling up the papers and sending them skittering away as if they'd grown legs.

While Millie chased pages into the back corners of the drawing room, Dermot busied himself kicking as much of it as he could under every table and chair he could reach. When she turned around, he stood with two handfuls, looking as sheepish as possible.

When, after closing the window, she got down on her hands and knees to gather pages together into piles, he knelt on the floor with her, pretending to help while actually spreading the mess whenever she looked away.

She sat back on her heels. "I'm going to call the servants. We need help."

"Oh, please don't." Dermot sat back as well. "I'm already banned from Baronsford after the Great Piglet Invasion. This will surely seal my fate on Heriot Row too. If this keeps up, I won't be allowed south of Aberdeen."

After bumping into her in Edinburgh and learning her plight, he'd set out to help her through a potentially difficult time, to brighten the dark moments he feared she was suffering through. And she'd barely left his thoughts for a moment since they parted.

"You're not banned from Baronsford. I learned later that you never even entered the ballroom."

"The tragic disaster involving a certain article of my clothing prevented me from indulging in the celebrated Pennington hospitality. And then, of course, there was the pig."

"Indeed. The pig." She rearranged her dress around her. She appeared perfectly comfortable seated as they were on the floor. "Incidentally, little Dermot was rescued just as the frightened creature emerged from beneath the skirts of a dowager duchess who, I understand, was highly entertained in spite of the uproar around her. By all reports, my father had to sit, he was laughing so hard. Cuffe and I decided afterwards not to admit to having any knowledge of the invader. And later on, no one seemed at all curious about where the pig came from."

"That may be due to the fact that I saw your sister and Wynne Melfort on my way out. I took full responsibility . . . and then dashed for the carriages before a vengeful mob could form."

"That showed wisdom, Dr. McKendry. We keep our pitchforks sharpened for such occasions."

He nodded his head graciously. "Thank you. My family is noted for its honorable retreats."

After leaving Millie's room, Dermot had sought out his partner and Lady Jo to make sure that no youngster on the estate would be blamed for the ruckus.

Millie picked up a few more pages within her reach.

A shaft of morning sun bathed her in a white glow, and Dermot stared. He'd known of Millie's beauty and engaging disposition long before his evening at Baronsford, but there were other things that drew his attention now. Her eyes were a magical shade of grey with flecks of silver. And she had a way of looking out from beneath her long, dark lashes that could make a man's heart race, but she was no seducer of men. He guessed the serenity of her disposition had allowed her to go unnoticed in social circles for much of her life.

She was slow to smile—with good reason, considering the news she'd recently received—but when her lips quirked at the corners, her entire face lit up, and in beauty, she rivaled Venus herself.

She inched over a little to gather pages from beneath a chair. A surgical drawing on one of them caused her to hesitate, and her expression darkened. He was wondering when she'd notice the topic of the lecture notes.

"Your sister Phoebe. Will she and Captain Bell be staying at Baronsford until the bairn comes?"

She looked up, immediately brightening like sunshine. "No, she'll be having the baby at Bellhorne Castle. They dropped me here yesterday on their way back to Fife. Neither of them wishes to leave Captain Bell's mother alone for any extended period of time. Phoebe is still a month away from delivering."

Dermot stretched his legs out, watching her. "I assume she'd want you with her, wherever she is, when the time comes?"

"There is my mother. And Jo. Of course, my brothers' wives are far more qualified."

"From what I understand, you're her closest friend. Lady Jo always brags the two of you as well could have been twins. You've always been inseparable, she told me. There's nothing that one of you goes through that the other is not part of."

Millie looked down and made a production of straightening the papers in her lap. "Were these pages in any order?"

"Unfortunately, they were. A precise order."

"And when did you say you needed to return them?"

"Today, if possible. My friend asked me to offer some comments on the lecture." Dermot looked about him and tried to give an impression of distress. "I know it's too much. I have no right to impose on your time . . ."

"Please ask."

"Might I organize the notes here? I've taken a room at Boyd's Inn, in White Horse Close, but the tavern has very bad lighting."

"I'd be delighted to help."

Dermot was relieved that he'd judged correctly. Perhaps, he'd hoped, she would find comfort in the familiar impulse of asserting some element of control on a world that had spun away from her.

Jumping to his feet, he extended his hand to help her up. Her soft, cool fingers nestled in his. His thumb caressed the softness before letting go. He was happy to see her face maintained a healthy hue. She directed him to a table where they could deposit the pages and work on either side.

"There's an index in this mess somewhere. If you don't mind, while you're putting the manuscript back together, I can peruse the content and consider what recommendations to make."

The notes *did* belong to a friend of his, but there was actually no urgency as to when to return them. They were from a series of lectures his colleague had given a few years ago, and Dermot had spent an hour this morning shuffling the pages out of order. His input would be pointless, of course. For more than a decade, he'd been serving in the Royal Navy and then establishing his hospital in the Highlands. But he'd sought out these notes specifically because the topic was particularly relevant to Millie's situation.

Despite his efforts to spread the notes as widely as possible in the room, he hated seeing her bending and picking them up.

"Why don't you start putting them in order and allow me to gather the rest?"

In a few moments, Dermot had piled them all on the designated table. A footman brought in tea and sandwiches, and they sat across from each other. Just as Dermot had hoped, collating the material required some scrutiny on her part, and she started asking questions.

"You said the lecturer is a friend of yours?"

"Indeed. Robert Liston. A young fellow who is pioneering a new school of thought in surgery."

"How are his methods different?" She was looking closely at page of anatomical sketches.

Dermot paused to gather his thoughts to say the right thing. He'd intended to raise her curiosity, and he didn't want to botch this opportunity.

"Liston advocates speed during surgical procedures. He believes this reduces pain, thus relieving strain on the patient. He's shown this has a direct impact on rates of survival."

Millie kept her gaze on the drawings.

"Other doctors connected with the university are pioneering new methods, as well. Surgeons like Archibald Drummond . . . and his wife, Isabella Murray Drummond, who is a German-trained physician *and* surgeon. Her father was a lifelong advocate of hygiene during surgery, and his studies show this effectively improves outcomes."

She casually laid the page down. "A female doctor?"

"She practices medicine in her husband's clinic on Infirmary Street, right here in Edinburgh."

Dermot tapped the papers on the table, trying hard not to reveal what he knew of her medical situation. Patience was called for here, he told himself. She had choices, and he wanted her to know what they were. Other physicians and surgeons in the city were far more qualified to provide the care she needed than the one she'd visited.

"I know you're quite busy, and I've already taken up too much of your time," he said. "But would you be interested in accompanying me to the Royal College of Surgeons this afternoon?"

She pushed the stack toward him. "For what reason?"

"I'd hazard a guess that it's like no place you've ever seen. Think of it as entertainment, in an odd way."

"I'm not sure."

"The college has a teaching museum used by students and alumni to better understand anatomical issues and aberrations. The public is not allowed in, but as a fellow there, I can take you through." He paused and laid his hand on the stack she'd put in order. "At the same time, I could return these."

"You don't need my company."

He sat back in his chair. "Well, the museum is famous for its superior organization of artifacts, and as re-organizing things seems to be of interest to you, I thought maybe this might give you some ideas. Of course, I may live to regret it."

"You're quite persuasive, Dr. McKendry. I believe I'll join you."

Chapter 5

Millie paused in the corridor outside the double doors. Above the entrance, the words ANATOMICALL THEATRE had been carved long ago in old-fashioned script in the dark wood.

The decision to accept the invitation and come had been made on impulse, but the Royal College of Surgeons was far more fascinating than Millie would have ever imagined. Upon arriving, she realized Dermot McKendry intended to introduce her to friends who held classes in the college, but Millie insisted they begin by going through the museum.

Dermot had already told her the old dissection theatre had housed the museum for as long as he knew. As he ushered her in, her attention was arrested by a framed, handwritten advertisement in a case, accompanied by an explanatory card. The cracked and yellowed paper had been inserted by the *Edinburgh Gazette* and was dated 16th September 1699.

> *These are to give notice that the Chirurgeon Apothecaries of Edinburgh are erecting a library of Physicall, Anatomicall, Chirurgicall, Botanicall, Pharmaceuticall and other Curious books. They are also making a collection of all naturall and artificiall curiosities. If any person have such to bestow let them give notice to Walter Porterfield present Treasurer to the Society at his home in the head of the Canongate who will cause their names to be honourably recorded and if they think not fit to bestow them gratis they shall have reasonable prices for them.*

Limbs, morbid specimens, diseased organs, abnormalities. Somewhat to her surprise, Millie found none of it disturbing, though the acrid smells permeating the air were like nothing she'd ever experienced.

"Preservation spirits." John William Turner, the Keeper of the Museum, breathed in deeply and shook his head. "I don't even notice it anymore."

Millie moved with Dermot from aisle to aisle, her curiosity aroused at every turn. Mr. Turner strolled alongside them, explaining in detail the long history of the museum and the plans for expansion. As they walked, the bespectacled young man had the air of a laird proudly showing off his estate.

Directors of institutions such as this always recognized the Pennington name, and Millie was accustomed to efforts to engage the family's interest in becoming a benefactor. Her parents and each of her siblings had their own projects, and she was involved with all of those. She'd always imagined the time would come when she too would find a cause she could sponsor. Someday.

Millie paused before a display of an amputated arm. *Someday* indicated an open-ended future she no longer possessed.

A brush of Dermot's hand against her shook Millie out of her gloomy thoughts. She glanced up at him and realized the touch was intentional. From the moment they'd walked in here, he'd been so aware of her, so attuned to her moods.

Mr. Turner was explaining how the young students used the specimen to understand the connection of tendons and ligament and bone. Then the museum curator pointed out a knee with a gunshot wound and an embedded musket ball mounted on the next table.

"Where did all these come from, Mr. Turner?"

"Many places, m'lady. Since the decision to begin the museum, we've been accepting and acquiring specimens from any number of sources," he explained. "The majority come from private collections, donated by the estates of former surgeons and professors who had assembled their own personal museums. Of course, some of the pieces have been rescued from the cupboards of the Royal Infirmary."

Having spent all her life in reasonably good health, there was so much that Millie didn't know about anatomy. But the libraries of Baronsford and their estate in Hertfordshire held many volumes on science and medicine, and because she was an avid reader, she was not completely ignorant of the illnesses that cut lives short.

Nearly three weeks ago, she'd first become aware of a heaviness in her right breast. The lump was palpable.

Right away she'd known, and the days following were lost in a nightmarish existence. Finally, determined to know for sure, she'd gone up to Edinburgh. Her suspicions were correct. The physician's diagnosis came at her like words spoken from some distance. *Cancer of the breast . . . perhaps a surgeon . . . very little hope.* She recalled only bits and pieces of what he said after that.

They passed by a long row of shelves displaying jawbones of various sizes. Two upright glass cases at the end held a dozen skulls in a variety of conditions.

Mr. Turner led them around a corner into another aisle. "And here in these bottles, we have twenty-three preserved examples of tumors of the breast."

Tumors of the breast. Millie's knees wobbled, and her steps faltered. She pressed a hand to her stomach. She couldn't tear her eyes from the squat glass jars, filled with small pieces of flesh in clear, yellowish liquid.

These had once been a part of living, breathing people. Women with families and dreams of a future. Was this all that remained of them? Had they moldered away to dust while these tumors that killed them remained here, preserved forever? Would part of her be here one day . . . in a jar with just a numbered card to identify her?

Dermot's arm wrapped around her waist. Millie needed him at that moment, and he was there. She leaned into him.

"Lady Millie has no need to see *every* specimen in the museum," he said sharply to Mr. Turner. He ushered her to a nearby window and pushed it open.

Breathing in the fresh air, she felt the weakness pass as quickly as it had descended.

The museum keeper hovered nearby. "I do hope I haven't overwhelmed her ladyship. I tend to get somewhat zealous in my enthusiasm, and I forget that lay folk —"

"I'm fine, Mr. Turner. Truly, I am."

Dermot was slow to release her.

She glanced back at the bottled specimens. In spite of her initial reaction, she wanted to look at them more closely. The unknown terrified her, and simply *seeing* them removed some of the mystery of this disease.

"Perhaps," Dermot suggested, "we should go outside. You can accompany me to the lecture halls, and I can return these notes to Dr. Liston."

"I'm quite recovered." Millie put a reassuring hand on his arm and looked into his eyes. He was still worried.

How serendipitous that he had come into her life at this moment. His kindness, his wit, his flair for the comic brought something into her world that she needed right now. It was as if heaven above had sent him to give her strength and clarity at a time when she needed both. Even bringing her here and showing her — without knowing it — that she was not alone in what she was facing. When had she ever met a man like him? Never.

"I'm at your disposal," Mr. Turner broke in. "Whatever you decide to do."

"Is there a library attached to the museum?"

"The museum does keep a collection of books for reference, of course. But I'm afraid we have no lending library."

"I meant, do you keep a catalogue of all these items?" She gestured to the aisles. "A summary of their history, perhaps."

Twenty-three breast tumor specimens seemed like so many. Did this indicate that the disease was common? Of all the women she'd known in her life, none had ever received the news she did. At least, none ever talked about it. She wanted to know more about these tumors and what had been the outcome for the patients.

"We do, m'lady." Mr. Turner gestured toward an open office door at the end of the hall. "My duties include keeping accurate records of the items we house. I can't affirm the earliest entries were recorded as faithfully as I attempt to do, but I'd be happy to show them to you."

"Wonderful." Millie turned to Dermot. "Dr. McKendry, if you have no objection, I'd like to stay here while you return the lecture notes to your friend."

He did object. She could tell by his darkened expression. "To be honest, I would not feel entirely comfortable leaving you alone, having brought you here."

"I'm certain if I faint dead away, I'll be quite safe," she teased, trying to ease his concern. "You don't have any piglets in these bottles, do you, Mr. Turner?"

"None, m'lady," the museum director replied, perplexed by the question.

"You see? I'll be fine, Doctor." She touched his hand. "You won't be gone too long, will you?"

"If you insist, I'll go." He bowed, acquiescing to her wishes. "And I'll return immediately."

She saw him glance back at her before he went out. If life were a fantasy and she had a tomorrow to dream of, Millie would choose to imagine that look as a next step in their relationship.

Mr. Turner escorted her to the office and seated her at his desk. Pulling the first of three oversized leather-bound ledgers from a bookshelf, he turned and then paused.

"Pardon me if I'm overstepping myself here, m'lady." He stared down at the volume in his hands and then smiled at her. "But after all Dr. McKendry has been through, it's quite gratifying to see his attentions fixed on a young lady again."

Millie felt her face flush. She saw no reason to explain that they were merely friends. That was all. But his comment piqued her curiosity.

"What do you mean, Mr. Turner, about what he's been through?"

Now he was the one to blush, and he went red from his collar to his scalp. "I don't know what I was thinking. I beg your pardon. I never should have mentioned it."

"But you have, and now you have me fretting. What did you mean about Dr. McKendry?" she asked again.

Her host was still hesitant, but Millie persisted until he explained. "My thoughtless words referred to his late fiancée. He lost her just as he was finishing his medical studies at the university."

Millie remembered everything her sister had said about Dermot. He wasn't looking for love. Jo heard him say he wished for no heir. He was committed to his hospital. His time was consumed by patients who needed his care and attention. Now Millie knew why.

"You say he lost her? How?"

"She killed herself just a few days before the wedding," Mr. Turner said gravely. "She'd been battling melancholia for quite some time, I understand."

To lose the person one loves at a time when the future appeared to be so bright. How heartbreaking for him.

Millie thought about her own future. She didn't know how this illness would affect her as it progressed, but she had an idea the end would not be pleasant. That was the reason she was traveling to America, to spare her family from a long period of pain, watching her decline when they should be thinking of babies and the new generation of Penningtons.

Dermot's fiancée had been fighting melancholia, that all-encompassing gloom that caused a person to waste away in darkness, unable to rouse herself from the depths of despair. At least, she had a man who loved her. That was something Millie had never known.

"How does one recover from such tragedy?" she murmured.

"Her death, understandably, hit him quite hard,. He closed down entirely. It was as if he too were dead. For his own safety, Dermot was committed to the asylum over in Livingston Yards."

Chapter 6

"Her ladyship is not at home, sir."

Dermot listened for some sign of Millie, but no sounds came from upstairs. The house was quiet as a church on Wednesday.

"Do you know when she'll be at home and receiving callers?"

"I can't say, sir."

The butler's stony face showed nothing, and Dermot knew he'd have better luck getting information from the flower arrangement at the center of the foyer. He could feel the eyes of the burly footman standing by the open door burning into his back.

Resigned, he turned down one corner of his card and dropped it on the silver tray in the butler's hand. A moment later, the front door closed behind him and he strode to the carriage. He didn't look back at the windows of the house.

He'd upset her, and he could kick himself. He'd done better getting her attention when he played the fool.

Taking her to the surgical museum was a mistake. His intention was for her to meet other doctors and know that here in Edinburgh, they were making huge strides in the advancement of medicine. But everything had gone terribly wrong.

The moment Turner pointed out the breast tumor specimens, her mood changed. The shock of seeing the bottles had affected her physically. He hadn't wanted to leave her after that, and he'd been a dolt to do so. By the time he'd returned from getting rid of the deuced lecture notes, she was downright dejected. Worry clouded her features, she would barely look at him, and her silence on the ride across town had been impenetrable.

He paused before climbing into the carriage. She was watching him now. He was certain of it. But he couldn't force his way in to talk to her. He wasn't about to give up, however. She needed someone, and he was the only one she had right now. She'd shut out her own family; he couldn't allow her to do the same to him.

His mind returned to the night of the ball at Baronsford. How she laughed. Truly laughed, as ridiculous as it all had been. In those few moments, she'd come alive, freed temporarily from any disquieting thoughts of the future. Clearly, she needed more gifts. Lively gifts.

The next day was Thursday. At dawn, Dermot sent the inn's stable boy off with a brilliant yellow canary in a small rattan cage. He was to wait within sight of the Pennington town house to make sure the gift was taken in. The sealed note on top was addressed to her.

For Lady Millie,

This pitiful creature has not uttered a note since I purchased him. I know, however, that under your tender care, listening to your cheery voice, this wee songbird shall,

"Like to the lark at break of day arising,
From sullen earth, sing hymns at heaven's gate."

Your Songless Friend

Receiving no response, he sent over another gift the following morning. This time, the lad delivered a cage containing a red squirrel with his note.

For Lady Millie,

Since purchasing this gift from a booth by St. Giles, I declare the creature has never once ceased showing me his teeth and glaring at me. And then I remembered thus,

*"The squirrel with aspiring mind,
Disdains to be to earth confined . . .
As Nature's wildest tenant free,
A merry forester is he."*

In your possession, this ball of red fur will surely have no greater aspiration but to serve as your smiling companion (as do I!), brightening your day and adding to your delight in the topiary gardens of Baronsford.

Your Earthbound Admirer

He wasn't sure if there was a topiary garden at Baronsford. But it didn't matter. Still, silence was the only response coming from Heriot Row.

Saturday, he decided to test her patience. After sending the lad off, he waited.

For Lady Millie,

I am sending you three of the scrawniest, most ornery chickens one might find in the stockyard near the Grass Market. However, I convey them to you with no doubt whatsoever that under your watchful care, they will become prize-winning birds at Melrose Village's next Michaelmas Fair (or perhaps the one after) and make you the envy of the Borders.

But my gift tomorrow will make you the toast of all Scotland.

Your Ardent Admirer

At midday, the burly footman who normally guarded the door at Heriot Row arrived with a letter. From the testy look on the man's face, Dermot decided his gifts were having some impact. The note confirmed it. The page looked like it had been left out in a summer rainstorm of black ink.

Dear Dr. McKendry,

Considering the havoc you have wreaked in my home, I feel you deserve [indecipherable blot] a far, far longer letter than [spatters of ink] this. But I'm presently too [blotted and crossed out word] irritated.

And, as you might have already surmised, I have broken my pen.

As I am now using my only remaining crow quill — and as I fear for its continuing safety in my hand — my response to you must be succinct.

Stop. I beg you. Stop.

Your Annoyed Former Friend
P.S. The squirrel has already bitten the butler twice.

Dermot held up the ink-stained paper and eyed it with satisfaction. He knew where Millie's writing desk sat. To the left, a large window opened out onto the garden in the rear of the house. To the right, the bookshelves that he'd "arranged" stood like a line of infantrymen along the wall. He liked to imagine her sealing this note to him with the hint of a smile on her lips.

Dermot knew these letters were stretching the rules of proper etiquette, but his conduct with Millie had been inappropriate from the first day they met. Social mores be damned. He sat to write out his reply.

Dearest Lady Millie,

I must profess I am at a loss as to whatever it is you accuse me. Please elaborate. Stop what, my lady?

In the meantime, I would be forever in your debt if I might call on you and renew our friendly acquaintance. This city, alas, is but a forlorn precipice of desolation . . . cold comfort without your fair company.

I remain, Humbly, Ever your friend, etc.

Dermot McKendry
P.S. How is my porcine namesake faring in the Borders? Send word quickly. I await your reply.

It was too much to hope she'd grace him with a second letter the same day. Not to be deterred, Dermot sent over another gift on Sunday morning. The stable boy returned and said he had to run for his life, for a "footman from hell" had nearly collared him as he put the cage on the front step.

Dermot's note read:

For Lady Millie,

Oh, bounteous day! I found this monkey for sale at a quayside shop in Leith and knew she MUST be yours. The previous owner has sworn on the beard of his great-grandfather's grandfather that she (the monkey, that is) will happily ride on your shoulder, whether in the park or on a stroll along Heriot Row.

Until you're able to train her to stop the incessant chattering (which I'm certain you'll be able to do in no time!), I do not recommend taking her to church services. Too much competition for the homilist, I should think.

Your Silent Friend

Millie didn't wait until noon to send a letter.

Sir,

I expect you here at Heriot Row Monday morning at the stroke of ten. If you do not come, and come promptly, then by all the righteous angels in heaven, I shall have a herd of elephants delivered to your inn door.

Millie

Dermot read the letter twice and caught his own smile reflected in the small mirror on the wall. "Finally, my invitation."

Stepping to the window, he pushed it open and leaned out. The stable boy was brushing down his next gift.

"Ahoy, laddie," he called down. "Return the llamas to Ducrow's Circus with my compliments. I'll not be needing them."

Chapter 7

"If I may be so bold as to ask once more, m'lady, are you *certain* you wish to do this?"

There was *one* thing Millie was quite sure of. This was the first time in all her twenty-six years that their butler in the Edinburgh town house had ever questioned her wishes. Or was it her sanity he was wondering about? She'd never done anything this outlandish, not even as a wee tot.

"I'm certain." She looked around the drawing room. The Persian carpets had been rolled up, and cloths had been draped over every chair, sofa, and table. Even the pictures hanging on the walls had been covered. She had no worries about any repercussions from her family. One of the benefits of spending her life conforming to every rule and regulation was that she'd earned the right to a little wildness.

If her rooms at Baronsford could be cleaned of the damage done by a greased pig, so could this drawing room.

"Bring them in here. All of them. Now."

"As you wish, m'lady." With a defeated look, the butler nodded to the footmen standing uncertainly by the doorway.

"And there will be an extra day's wages for everyone who helps put the room to rights later," Millie said. She immediately heard murmurs of approval behind her as she closed the last window.

The cages were carried in and placed on the floor. After sending the servants out, she started to free her new companions. The canary immediately took flight, circling the room and fluttering up against every window before landing on top of a covered painting on the wall. The bird was truly the most silent songbird in creation, and she looked at Millie now with the same doubtful expression the butler had been wearing.

Upon her release, the squirrel became a russet-colored blur, racing about the room, leaping on and off the furniture. Espying the tray of refreshments, in the blink of an eye the creature was on the table, sitting back on her haunches and stuffing walnuts into her cheeks as fast as she possibly could.

Millie proceeded to release the three chickens next. They were truly the most pitiful birds in creation. Looking at them now, scraggly and thin, with patches of feathers missing entirely, she had no doubt about why they'd gone unsold at the market. They strutted about, soiling the dark wood floor and clucking and pecking at furniture cloths and each other.

The monkey quieted down the moment the cage was opened. Clearly seeing herself as superior to the rest of the animals, the little mammal climbed calmly up Millie's arm and sat on her shoulder, holding on to the collar of her dress and eyeing the rest with benign disdain.

Millie felt the same pang of regret she'd had yesterday after sending her note to Dermot, demanding today's meeting. She should have held off, for she was curious to know what other companions he might have sent her.

As a man and a doctor, Dermot McKendry had fascinated her since before she ever met him. It was not just the stories Jo told her or the initial state of his office. He had an absolutely wicked sense of humor. This latest foolishness was tremendously endearing and totally unexpected. Since the arrival of her menagerie, she'd had no time to think. No time to wallow in the gloom of her situation. These past few mornings, she'd opened her eyes with a sense of expectation, hurrying downstairs to discover what new gift had been delivered.

To Millie's surprise, the canary trilled for the first time a moment before the knock came at the front door. She glanced toward the clock just as it chimed the hour.

Dermot was, of course, on time.

Whatever expectations or misgivings he'd had about how his mischief had affected Millie, they were cast to the wind the moment Dermot entered the drawing room. She'd kept all of his gifts, and they were running freely about the room.

"Close the door. Quickly! We can't allow them to escape now, can we?"

Formality was forgotten. The footman backed out immediately, and Dermot turned in time to have a yellow bird fly at his face. He gently tried to shoo it away, but the canary seemed to have a mind of its own.

"I believe she's the angriest of all." Millie stretched out her hand, and the bird landed on it. "She did, however, sing for the first time only a moment ago."

Millie was a vision from a fairy tale. She was dressed in white with a monkey on her shoulder and a bird perched on her finger. Her hair was in slight disarray. Her cheeks glowed pink. He wished he had some artistic talent, for this was an image that needed to be painted and admired. He quickly dismissed the thought; he could never capture the vibrant essence of her personality on canvas.

"The canary is a she?" he finally asked. He didn't have the heart to tell her only the male bird sings.

"They're all female. I imagined you knew that."

She motioned to a table holding the tray of sandwiches and pastries and such. The red squirrel sitting on the tray grabbed the last walnut from a dish and scampered off.

"No excuses today, Dr. McKendry. You're joining us for refreshments."

"Ouch." He looked down at the chickens pecking viciously at his trousers. "Get away."

"Reason with them. Tell them it's your fault the cook has tied a different color ribbon to their feet to identify the day they're to go into the stew."

He noticed the ribbons. She wasn't jesting. "Perhaps they should be fattened up a wee bit first."

"You're right." She encouraged the canary to sit on an unlit lamp and led the way toward the table. "I'll speak to the cook about it."

Dermot moved cautiously, with the clucking chickens weaving between his legs and continuing to peck at him. "Stop! Is this any way to treat the man who delivered you here? There are far more ignominious fates than ending up as Lady Millie's dinner…though at the moment, I can't think of one."

Millie stopped and faced him. "So you admit these gifts came from you?"

He bowed. "You've caught me out. I may have had *something* to do with it."

As his hostess proceeded toward the table, he frowned at the monkey who was perched on her shoulder and sticking out its tongue at him.

Millie sat, and he joined her. With a little nudge, the monkey climbed down and followed the squirrel, who had returned and was pawing through a plate of sandwiches.

"Would you care for one, Doctor?"

The red squirrel lifted her face, both cheeks stuffed full. The monkey paused as well and glared, a sandwich held in each hand. The warning was clear.

"I'm fine."

"Coffee, then?" She poured out a cup and handed it across the table.

Dermot was about the take a sip when the yellow bird flew across the room and landed on his shoulder. It trilled prettily in his ear, and he began to think he hadn't chosen too badly—in this case, at least—when the feathered rodent flew away, leaving a spot on his blue coat.

He put the cup down.

"Is something wrong?" she asked.

The hens were at his feet again, this time going at his boots. When one attacked his knee, however, Dermot reached down, grabbed the offender, and tossed it over his shoulder. It sailed off in an indignant flutter of feathers and squawks, the red ribbon trailing behind. "Nothing at all."

The canary flew back and perched on his other shoulder. Obviously, it was not finished. Looking him in the eye, it crooned a few low notes and then flew off, leaving its mark there, as well, as he'd anticipated. Perhaps it was a 'she', after all.

"Are you finding my little friends to be a nuisance?"

"Not at all." The chickens were back, pecking away with a vengeance. He shook his napkin at them and crossed his legs.

"Are you comfortable, Dr. McKendry?"

"Absolutely," he lied.

"And enjoying yourself?"

"Absolutely." At that moment, the red-ribboned hen jumped up on his knee, digging in with her sharp talons. "How could I not be?"

When he batted the bird away, the squirrel leapt off the table and ran through his legs, and the monkey stood on the tray and screeched in support. The canary was back, this time landing on top of his head, pecking at his scalp.

"Bloody hell!"

Dermot jumped to his feet, his hands and feet moving simultaneously as he tried to ward off the assailants.

"Excuse my outburst," he managed to get out between defensive maneuvers. "But how ever did you train them in such a short time?"

"I don't know what you mean," she said innocently, calmly watching as if nothing were amiss. "You *do* live in the Highlands, Doctor, do you not?"

He caught the hint of a smile on her lips. He'd brought these beasts to her door, but it was her eyes that danced with mischief.

"The last time I visited the Abbey, I walked through the farms. Working farms. I can't understand why you'd be so troubled by an animal or two."

"Very well. I'll say it. I apologize for afflicting you with this plague of wild things."

Then, as suddenly as they began, the animals lost interest in him. The chickens wandered off, the squirrel and the monkey resumed their breakfast, and the canary flew to the top of the clock, where it began to sing.

Dermot shook his head and sat down again, returning Millie's smile.

She tilted her head toward the door. "I'll be sure to pass on your apologies to the staff. The housekeeper was ready to resign her post last night. And the butler thinks I've gone mad. The maids run away and hide whenever the footman opens the front door."

Dermot eyed the chicken with the red ribbon warily. She was peering at him from behind

Millie's chair. He would offer his own apologies on the way out. He didn't know how to tell her exactly, but chaos wasn't the only result he'd wanted to achieve. Her raised spirits were the thing he'd hoped for, and her bright face told him he hadn't miscalculated.

"First the piglet. And then these animals." She waved at the creatures around them. "Why did you go to such trouble?"

Millie's question was direct, and it helped him. Perhaps the time had come to speak candidly. He reached out to pick up his cup, saw the warning looks on the faces of the monkey and the red squirrel, and thought better of it.

"I know it was not your intention to raise the stakes on the pranks we've been playing on each other." She folded her napkin and smoothed it over her lap. "And I know you're not doing it to court me. There's something else."

He *wished* his actions had been an attempt to court her, but he pushed the thought away.

Dermot was a master at maneuvering a person's thinking to calm them or to challenge them. The years spent in his profession had equipped him with invaluable tools that he could employ to help someone afflicted with grief or melancholy or some other state of mental distress. And many times this past week, he'd thought of this very moment. But suddenly, his mind had gone blank. He could only speak from his heart.

"My intention was to distract you."

"Distract me?" She was surprised. "Why?"

"Because I know what you're going through right now."

She started to respond but stopped. The cup moved slowly to her lips. He didn't want his words to undo whatever ground she'd gained these last few days. Go slowly, he told himself.

"What is it *exactly* that you know, Dr. McKendry?" she finally asked, putting the coffee cup down on the table.

It was not possible to evade her questions, even if he wanted to. Directness defined the way she lived her life. The way she saw the world. Dermot was the same. "I ran into you — or rather, you ran into me — a few days before the ball at Baronsford. It was in a lane above Cowgate. You were too upset to look up, but I recognized you."

Her eyes closed momentarily, and she massaged her temples. She was looking for a plausible way to explain her being there. But he didn't want any more fabrications muddying the waters between them.

He reached inside his pocket and took out the card that he'd been carrying around since that day. "You dropped this when you were giving your money to some children in the lane. It's Dr. Jessen's card."

She glanced at it and shook her head. "You must be mistaken. I did walk in Cowgate once during that week but—"

"Don't, Millie," he said softly, tossing formality aside. "I *know*. I went to speak with him . . . as a physician. He told me the difficult news he'd had to deliver to the young woman who just left his office."

Her chin lifted. Her eyes were wide and frightened. Dermot wanted to move to her side, take her into his arms, tell her that all would be well.

"Who have you told?"

"No one. Your decisions, your choices, are for you alone to make. I would never undermine you in that," he said with passion, meaning every word. "It was as a friend and as someone in the medical profession that I took the liberty of trying to distract you and to make you aware of options that are open to you."

"Bringing the lecture notes about surgical procedures was part of your plan."

"It is an option that's available that Dr. Jessen might not have discussed with you. And there are excellent surgeons in Edinburgh. I told you about Dr. Isabella Drummond because she is always referred to in the highest terms and she's a woman."

"You took me to the museum, to the Royal College of Surgeons."

"I wanted you to meet other doctors. Jessen is a fine physician, but he is not close to the best for treating a patient with your condition." His voice shook, but he tried to keep his tone convincing. "Your life is at stake, Millie. You can't trust one person and one opinion. You have the means to —"

"What if no one can help me?"

Susan's face appeared in his mind's eye, and like ashes caught up in the wind, the image disintegrated, whirled, and flew away. Dermot hadn't helped her. He hadn't known how, and he'd made a mistake. This was now, he told himself. He'd grown. He had far more knowledge, more connections. And he needed Millie to trust him.

"Someone *will* help you. I'll help you. There is a way, and we'll find it."

Her eyes glistened as she leaned toward him. "Thank you."

Her hand stretched across the table. He took it in his own. Her fingers were cold, and they clutched his tightly. He couldn't let her die. He wouldn't allow it to happen.

"I'm grateful to what you've done, and for your friendship, but right now, I need time," she whispered, taking her hand back. "Time to think."

He understood, but he also felt like a failure. He had so much more on his mind that he wanted to share. She mattered to him. More than as a friend, or as his partner's sister-in-law. Millie had become essential to him. She'd filled a gaping hole in his heart that had lingered there for years.

"Millie."

"It's all right. But please, right now, I need you to leave me."

The door closed behind Dermot, and her tears welled up and overflowed. Millie sat on the edge of the chair as her sobs overtook her. She wasn't alone. She didn't have to go through the illness on her own.

The monkey climbed onto her shoulder and put her arms around her neck.

Millie laughed through her tears, petting the little animal.

Dermot knew her secret. He cared. He was affected by what she was going through. He had hope when she didn't dare to have any. She wiped her face and tried to calm herself. She wanted to share some of the weight she'd been carrying for the past few weeks with him.

But she couldn't do this to him; Mr. Turner's words kept coming back to her.

Dermot had loved, and he'd lost. He'd suffered badly, to the point of being committed to an asylum.

She could feel his affection for her. If she accepted his help, would he be hurt once again? She could not forgive herself if her own affliction caused him pain.

And what about her? Would she be satisfied if he helped her as a family friend . . . remaining impartial? She cared for him too much already. Tears streamed down her cheeks. She had no answers.

Chapter 8

The horse's hooves rang out on the granite cobblestones of Heriot Row, raising sparks as the rider from Bellhorne reined in his mount and vaulted to the pavement in front of the Pennington town house. As he banged on the door, rousing the footman and the rest of the household, the bells atop St. Andrew's a few blocks away pealed out the hour of three.

Handing off his message for Lady Millie, he was back on his horse in minute and racing through the murky predawn light toward Baronsford.

The message from Captain Bell was clearly rushed and relayed very little information, except to tell her that Phoebe had already started feeling labor pains, and she wanted her sister with her.

Millie cried, she laughed, and then she felt the urge to get on the road immediately. As her maid helped her dress and pack, she called for a driver and footmen to have a carriage ready. When the housekeeper ordered the maid out to prepare for the trip, Millie stopped her. She wouldn't be taking her. She had another plan.

An hour later, the carriage clattered up to the entrance of White Horse Close. One of her footmen offered to take a message into the inn for her. But she wouldn't have it. She cared nothing about society's rules now. What did reputation matter when there was no certainty of tomorrow?

It was well past four in the morning when she rapped on Dr. McKendry's door, and he pulled it open. Her heart skipped at the sight of him, bathed in the dawn light coming in the window in his room. Untidy hair, drowsy eyes, his shirt open and exposing a muscular chest. His trousers hung low on his hips, and his feet were bare.

He became immediately alert as soon as he saw her. "Millie, what's wrong?"

"I know it's completely inappropriate to come here. And I understand I have no right to ask this of you, that I'm abusing our relationship."

"What is it? Tell me. Ask anything."

"Phoebe is in labor. She wants me with her in Fife. The babe is coming early." Panic washed through her, and the words came tumbling out. "What if something goes wrong? What if everything goes wrong? I'm frightened. I think I'm going mad. Sad thoughts . . . horrible thoughts . . ."

Millie didn't realize she was shaking until Dermot pulled her into his embrace and she felt his muscular arms around her. He caressed her back and shoulders, whispering reassuring words in her ear. She pressed her cheek against his warm chest, breathing in his scent and holding him as he held her.

"She needs me. But I'm filled with terrible doubts. I expect the worst. I don't think I'm strong enough to go to her."

His chin brushed against her hair. "You're her sister. And you *are* strong. Plenty strong. And you'll fight the battles that need to be fought. Slay the monsters that threaten. You'll do everything you need to do. You'll go there and stand beside her and hold her hand and support her. She'll get through the childbirth, and all will be well. Think it. Believe it. All will go well."

Phoebe's beautiful face appeared in her mind's eye. Phoebe the writer. Phoebe the danger seeker. Phoebe the opinionated sister who was different from Millie in personality and temperament. And yet, they were like two halves of a whole. Where one erred, the other mended. Where one slipped, the other kept them on solid ground. They loved and complemented each other.

As recently as a year ago, where one went in the world, the other followed. Then Phoebe married Captain Ian Bell, and life had changed for both of them. It was the natural progression, and Millie had embraced it with happiness. Now, she only wished the child would come into this world without difficulty, that it would bring joy and laughter to Bellhorne, where they'd been absent for so long. The Bell family had been in mourning for a long time, ever since Ian's younger sister Sarah had been lost to them.

Tonight, however, the focus was on Phoebe. Millie agreed with everything Dermot said. And whatever she was going through with her own health, it had no business intruding on what needed to be done for her sister.

He drew back, tilting her face upward. His thumbs brushed away the wetness on her cheeks. "Better?"

"Much," she whispered. He was a gift. His words were what she needed to hear. "You're the only one who knows what I'm going through. The only one who understands."

He caressed the line of her cheek. His eyes studied her, as if he was branding into his memory this moment. Millie wished she could stay here, gathered in his arms, forever. How easy it would be to press her lips against his, to run her fingers on his skin, to close the door behind them and shut out the world.

But her sister needed her.

"My carriage is waiting. And I know . . . it's a hardship, an inconvenience . . . but would you consider coming with me to Fife?" She drew in her breath and held it, realizing the imposition of such a favor. "I'm sorry. I should never have—"

"I'm honored that you ask me. Wait for me downstairs. I'll be right down."

The ten easy miles from Edinburgh to Queensferry passed in absolute silence, for Millie sat with her arm tucked into his and her head against Dermot's shoulder. He was pleased she was able to find comfort enough from him to sleep. She'd drifted off even before Castle Hill had dropped out of sight behind them.

Dermot watched the flat and rolling fields and villages and the occasional ruined tower house as the rising sun cast shadows against the front wall of the carriage. He kept telling himself that attraction didn't need to evolve into affection. Caring for someone could exist independently of love. It was only logical.

The rawness of his emotions told him, however, that he was far too late for such quibbling. His feelings toward her had been changing, deepening. Each time they met only served to bring them closer, building on a foundation that was laid before they were even introduced.

But it was the disease afflicting her that was making him frantic. He was more than worried, he was becoming desperate. Each day, she came one step closer to being too late. He was a surgeon. He knew that timeliness was critical. He understood the dangers she faced, but something needed to be done. She had decisions she needed to face. And yet, he couldn't force her to do anything. He certainly wouldn't tell her family, regardless of the fact that Wynne and her sister Jo were his closest friends.

He'd made that mistake before, and it led to Susan taking her own life.

The Firth of Forth was smooth for the ferry crossing, and ahead of them, the skies over Fife were clear. Standing beside Millie, he hid his concerns, telling himself he was here for her. What he alone could offer had to suffice. It was the way she wished it. How he felt about her, the fears that plagued him, needed to be kept in check. They were secondary to her desires.

In anticipation of Millie's arrival, Captain Bell had a carriage waiting for them at the ferry dock for the remaining sixteen miles of their journey.

She sat beside him, as before, her head against his shoulder, her bonnet on the seat across from them. She was so at ease with him that his heart swelled. They'd been following the coast road for quite some time when Dermot looked over and saw she was awake. He brushed his chin against the softness of her hair. Her hand slipped into his, and the way their fingers entwined spoke of more than friendship. Suddenly, he felt a burn in the back of his throat.

"Have you thought over any of the suggestions I made yesterday?"

She rubbed her cheek against his coat and stayed silent.

"If you'll allow me, I can make arrangements for you to meet several surgeons. Good ones. You can choose the one you want."

A second hand rested on his sleeve. She was staring out the side window.

"Millie." He pressed her hand. "Talk to me. Tell me you're considering it."

She lifted her face and looked up at him. He saw the tears welling up, saw the trembling lip.

"As friends. You must promise me. You'll not care for me more than you would for any mere friend."

"Oh, sweetheart, it's far too late for that," he replied, then leaned forward to kiss her.

Millie wanted this, but she feared it. Her body and her heart ached to be in Dermot's arms, but her mind charged her to remember his past and his loss.

Unfortunately, he was right. It was far too late.

His lips pulled away as if sensing her hesitation, but she was not about to let him go. Millie raised herself and kissed him again. A fire was racing through her, immolating all vestiges of reason. She wanted him.

She moved in his arms, trying to get closer to his body. He lifted her and set her on his lap. Her hands moved over his shoulders, his back. Her mouth sought his and found it.

As he kissed her again, she opened for him. He groaned his approval. His tongue was searching, tasting. She wanted more. She'd never experienced passion, but she knew it could be all-consuming. And she wanted to be consumed. She needed him.

Millie's hands moved inside his coat and waistcoat. She wanted to tear open his shirt, feel the hot skin she'd pressed her face against when she'd come for him at the inn.

She shifted restlessly in his lap, feeling him rise hard against her. His hands took hold of her waist, and he broke off the kiss.

"Millie, I'm falling too quickly."

She moved again. "Then fall. Please fall. And take me with you. Show me."

Dermot's hands framed her face, and he looked into her eyes. "I can't. I won't take advantage of you. Not when you're like this."

"Like what?"

"When you're so vulnerable."

"Is this vulnerable?" Millie kissed him again. This time, she tried to pour all the longing she felt tearing at her into the heated press of lips, into the primal dance of their tongues. "I want you, Dermot."

His reaction was immediate. His arms tightened around her, his mouth as greedy as her own as he gave as much as he took. Millie clung to him, teetering on the edge of sanity as he caressed and molded her dress against her body. Every inch of her body was alive.

But when she expected more, he pulled back slightly. "Will you still want me tomorrow?"

"I will," she promised, floating in a haze.

"And the day after?"

She brushed her lips against his. "I will."

"Will you want me next month?"

Now it was her turn to draw back a little, and she saw the sadness in his eyes. Tears welled and rolled down her cheeks. She pressed her forehead to his. She understood what he was asking.

"I will."

"Then you must fight this . . . for me. And you must allow me to fight it with you. The two of us will claw our way through, forge a path for our future, however hard it might be."

Millie wrapped her arms around him and buried her face against his shoulder.

She wanted that future. She wanted everything he asked for. But she was afraid.

Chapter 9

Millie and Dermot were greeted with good news as soon as the carriage rolled to a stop at Bellhorne Castle. Sarah Pennington Bell had entered the world just before dawn, at nearly the same time the rider arrived in Edinburgh to deliver Ian Bell's letter.

Dr. Thornton, who'd delivered the baby, grudgingly interrupted the breakfast he was eating in the dining room to give Millie a full report. Though he was hardly her favorite of all the people attached to Bellhorne, the family doctor seemed far less brusque and impertinent than she remembered. According to Phoebe, his manners and temperament had been improving steadily since his marriage to Captain Bell's cousin, Alice Young.

Even so, in his inimitable way, Thornton announced the bairn's lungs were strong and her temper was a match of her mother's. The wee lass and Phoebe were doing wonderfully. Captain Bell, however, might need a day or two to recover his strength. Millie was certain she'd never heard the man joke before. She left Dermot in the company of the doctor and his wife, who was on hand to help. Thornton was happy to meet another medical man.

A few minutes later, Millie tapped on her sister's door and entered, hearing Phoebe's voice. She didn't know if she should laugh or cry at the sight she walked in on. Naturally, she did both.

Phoebe was propped up in bed with pillows tucked around her. She looked tired, but she beamed with happiness at the sight of Millie. A portable writing desk was balanced on her lap, and Millie had no doubt she was already writing about the ordeal of childbirth. Next to her, Ian was sound asleep, holding his precious napping daughter in the crook of his arm.

"Can you believe it? She's here." Phoebe put the desk on a side table and opened her arms.

Millie moved into her sister's embrace. A mother. Her sister was a mother. The worst of Millie's worry was behind them. Phoebe and the baby girl were healthy. Despite what Phoebe had to go through, she seemed in exceptionally good spirits. She drew back to look into her sister's face again and tucked away the strands of dark curls.

"Are you truly well?"

"Never been better." Phoebe smiled at her husband and touched the tiny fist poking up from the swaddling. The little fingers were perfect. "We named her Sarah."

"I'm certain Ian's sister is smiling down on all of you right now. I didn't see Mrs. Bell — the *senior* Mrs. Bell — downstairs to congratulate her. I know she must be pleased, as well."

"She's quite happy." Phoebe sighed. "She was with me, holding my hand the whole time. I had to beg her to get some rest before our family arrives."

Millie adjusted the blankets on her sister's lap. "I suspect you'll have everyone at your door tomorrow."

Phoebe touched Millie's cheek. "But you came right away."

"I was closest. First to receive the news."

"Did you travel alone?"

"Actually, I came with Dr. McKendry."

Phoebe's squeal caused Ian to stir, and the baby jumped. The sisters stared, holding their breaths as the infant made little mewling sounds before settling back to sleep.

"So . . . Dr. McKendry!" Phoebe asked in a hushed tone. "When did you two finally meet? He was supposed to come to the ball."

Jo and Wynne and Cuffe were the only ones in the family who knew Dermot had been there. And none of them, including Millie, had said anything about it.

"He called on me in Edinburgh."

"No wonder you were so anxious to go back up to the city." Phoebe adjusted her position and winced.

"Was it very difficult?" she asked. "The birth, I mean."

Millie helped her slide down a little.

"Not at all," Phoebe scoffed, wincing again. "Nothing to it."

When she was settled, the two of them gazed at the baby—the new mother with a look of contentment and love, Millie with a sense of awe.

Phoebe took hold of Millie's hand. "Do you know for an entire year Jo and I have been trying to get you two to meet?"

Her matchmaking sisters. Millie knew. She'd been hoping for the same thing. But fate would have it that when they finally met, it would be under quite singular circumstances.

"You look pale. You've been crying. What's wrong?"

"Nothing is wrong," Millie lied. "Only a little tired. I've been on the road for much of the night."

Phoebe tugged on her hand. "Well, tired or not, tell me about our good doctor. What do you think of him?"

"I think very highly of him." Millie smiled.

"You must, or you wouldn't have brought him along." She nudged her. "How many times has he called on you? I need details." Phoebe's eyebrows went up and down suggestively.

Her sister never changed. That was one of the thousand reasons Millie loved her so much.

"I'm not giving up without a fight, miss. Has he kissed you?"

"Phoebe!"

"Have you kissed him back?"

Millie recalled the last leg of their ride and their kiss. "You, Mrs. Bell, are a married woman now. And a mother. Behave yourself and get some rest."

"That means *yes*." Phoebe tilted her head knowingly. "Has he sent you any gifts? That's a definite sign, you know, when a suitor sends gifts."

Millie said nothing but smoothed out the bedclothes around her sister. If Phoebe only knew . . .

"You two were alone in Edinburgh for days and days. I hope you made the most of your time. But I can see I'll need to be writing to the staff on Heriot Row to get the facts."

"Phoebe! You're incorrigible. Seriously!" She gestured meaningfully toward the man sleeping on the far side of the bed and shook her head.

"As you wish. I'll let you off for the moment, but we're not done discussing this."

"I believe we are finished, you monster."

Phoebe took her hand. "Well, after all your courting, it's your duty to ask him to marry you."

"My duty?" She laughed.

"You're an earl's daughter with the large dowry, and you know that can be intimidating for any man who's not a fortune-hunter. And we don't want to let a good one get away. But I'll not say another word about it . . . for now."

Millie thought about Dermot. Somehow, between rearranged bookshelves and voracious squirrels, she'd fallen in love with him. But before they could ever talk about marriage, she needed to tell him what she knew of his past, his fiancée, and his time in the asylum.

"When can I steal my niece?" Millie said, standing and changing the subject. Right now, she didn't want to think about the future. She only wanted to enjoy this moment. "I'm dying to hold her."

Phoebe looked over at her husband and daughter and smiled. "Stealing her? You'll have to take on Captain Bell. I don't think he's *ever* going to let her out of his sight."

In many ways Bellhorne Castle reminded Dermot of the Abbey, his own home in the Highlands. People came and went. They contributed where it was needed. And they just belonged.

Captain Bell's mother seemed to be a combination of Dermot's aunt and Jo's real father, Charles Barton...kindness and moments of forgetfulness wrapped in one loving person. As the afternoon slipped by toward dinner, the old woman asked Dermot variations of the same question half a dozen times.

Oh, my dear, have we been introduced?

To whom do you belong, sir?

When were you and Lady Millie married?

It was during one of those moments when Bell came to Dermot's rescue. "Dr. McKendry, allow me to escort you to the library. Lady Millie is waiting there."

"Thank you." With a bow to Mrs. Bell, he excused himself. He hadn't seen Millie since they arrived, though he knew she'd been busy visiting with her sister.

"I hope you'll forgive my mother's tendency to become . . . unfocused at times," Bell said as they climbed the stairs from the Great Hall to a gallery.

"Please, think no more about it. She's a lovely woman."

"I'm familiar with your work at the Abbey, and I admire what you and Captain Melfort have been able to accomplish. But my mother is different and—"

"I understand. I know her condition started after your sister's disappearance. But I hear it's much improved in this past year." Dermot knew his profession sometimes made people defensive. Diseases of the mind were not very well understood, and fear was often the result. But he wasn't in the business of recruiting patients to his hospital. He gently elaborated on this on their way.

The captain was pleased to talk to him about it. He took him only as far as the door. "I've already warned Millie that I'll let out the guard dogs if she tries to escape with my daughter." He smiled. "You are in charge, McKendry. Make sure she causes no trouble."

"I'll do my best."

Dermot entered the library and came to an immediate halt. He took a moment to enjoy the scene before him and another moment to find his voice.

Millie sat in a corner of the bright, well-appointed room. Shafts of golden sunlight spread across the floor. She'd kicked off her slippers, and her legs were stretched out on a sofa. Her face was bent over a precious bundle in her arm. Some of her soft brown hair had come free and tendrils hung loose, as they had the first night he saw her at Baronsford. She lifted her face and looked at him, and Dermot knew he was a lost man.

"Come." She smiled. "Come and meet her."

She swung her feet to the floor, and he sat next to her.

"Isn't she the most beautiful creature you've ever seen?"

"Indeed, she is." Mille *was* the most beautiful creature. He managed to tear his gaze from her and look down at the wide-eyed infant.

The bairn opened her mouth and stuck her tongue out at him. She knew he hadn't been truthful.

"I believe that's a sign of genius when an infant sticks her tongue out."

"I'm certain you're right," he said, admiring the plump cheeks and light-colored wisps of hair.

"She is small, but sturdy. Look at these little fingers. Even the fingernails. So perfect."

He agreed. Dermot touched the tiny fingers, and they stretched for him. He traced the pale, arched eyebrows. The soft, smooth forehead. Little Sarah blinked as if satisfied with his attention now.

"I'll never experience this, will I?" she asked, her voice choked with tears. "I can't be a mother, can I?"

Millie's words threatened to rip out his heart. Dermot forced his way out of the abyss of sadness and found his voice.

"There is nothing you can't do," he whispered, brushing his lips across her temple. "Have faith, my love."

Chapter 10

Millie knew that once her parents arrived at Bellhorne, her time wouldn't be her own. She had things she needed to say to Dermot.

The next morning, when he came downstairs, she was waiting for him. Leading him through the gardens, she took him out into the fields and through the deserted nomad's camp to the path that ran along the shaded brook.

"Where are we going?"

"You'll see." Millie had taken these paths many times when she was younger. Ian's sister always led the way.

Sarah's murder had been devastating for so many people, including Phoebe, who had been particularly close to her. Then fate had taken a hand, crossing the paths of Phoebe and Ian in the vaults beneath Edinburgh's Old Town. The dangers that followed had nearly cost the lives of others but had ended happily.

"They call this forest the Auld Grove. In a glen not far from here, there's a group of deserted stone buildings where Ian rescued my sister after she was pushed into a well." She pulled off her bonnet and waved it in that direction.

"So, this is the place." Dermot looked around him. "I heard some of the story from Dr. Thornton and his wife yesterday. Terrifying for all of you."

"I'm sorry I abandoned you for so long."

He smiled. "I know my limits. I can never compete with that bonnie bairn for your attention." He took her hand. "On a more serious matter, you're not taking me out here to push me into that well, are you?"

"I might be."

Not far ahead, they came to the waterfall in the glen. Then, beyond a short, steep rise, they reached an open meadow bordered by thick forest. In the center stood an ancient stone circle.

"I love this place," she whispered.

They stood together in the summer sunshine, surrounded by patches of bluebells bobbing their tiny heads. She let go of his hand, and he moved inside the perimeter of the standing stones.

"Sarah used to say that people come from all over Scotland to make pilgrimages here." The stones were weathered, and some had fallen, but the circle was largely intact.

"I've seen others like this. In Orkney and Shetland. On the Isle of Lewis." He touched each stone in turn, moving slowly from one to the next, running his fingers over grooves carved by the passage of years. "I can imagine witches and sorcerers performing rituals of the auld religion here on moonlit nights."

As he spoke, she was reminded that he was a Highlander. The history and culture of this land was part of him.

"So I was correct." He stood by a rude stone table at the center. "You plan to sacrifice me on this altar for the gifts I sent you in Edinburgh."

"I have other plans for you." She motioned him to come toward the ravine. Below them, the waterfall tumbled over moss-covered rocks, and a cool mist hung in the air. She walked along the edge until they reached the particular shrub she was looking for.

"White heather!" he exclaimed.

She bent down and touched the tender blooms. "You know the legend?"

"What Highlander didn't hear it at his grandmother's knee?"

"I only know the story from books."

He crouched beside her, and Millie admired the play of the wind in his hair. She stared at his lips, and in her mind she was back in the carriage, kissing him. Then, she was in the library when she burst into tears and he held her, the infant nestled safe and snug between them.

His fingers brushed against Millie's as he swept it across the white flowers. "Tell me what you know."

"I read the tale in James Macpherson's book of Ossian."

He sat beside the heather and pulled her down next to him.

"Ossian had a beautiful daughter, Malvina," she began, "and she was pure of heart and very beautiful."

"She was betrothed to Oscar, the strongest and most courageous of warriors," he finished for her. "But before you continue, I warn you not to think of the two of them having anything in common with us. The tale is too sad."

She agreed. She wouldn't. "One day, when summer was drifting into autumn, Oscar was away at war but due to return. In the distance, she saw a figure limping toward her through the heather."

"Oscar's faithful messenger, wounded in battle," Dermot added.

"The man knelt before Malvina and gave her a sprig of heather that Oscar had plucked as he lay mortally wounded, waiting for death. He sent it as a token of his undying love."

Millie's gaze lifted and met Dermot's.

"As she listened, tears fell from Malvina's eyes, and the purple heather turned white," he continued for her. "Afterwards, as Malvina walked over the moors, her tears turned the blossoms white wherever they fell."

Millie didn't know she was crying until Dermot reached up and tenderly brushed her tears away.

"Even in her sadness, she wished for the happiness of others." Millie paused and could not continue. A knot the size of a fist had risen into her chest, and she couldn't get the words out.

Dermot finished it for her, but his voice, too, was thick with emotion. "She prayed that the white heather, a symbol of her sorrow, would bring good fortune to all who find it."

He leaned toward her, kissing the wetness from one cheek, then the other.

"Here is the white heather, Millie. Make your wishes. Believe in the magic."

She cried and smiled at the same time, and then plucked off a bloom. "That Phoebe and her daughter should continue to thrive."

Dermot broke off a sprig of white flowers. "That the union of the Pennington and Bell families strengthen them both."

"That joy dwell in the halls of Bellhorne Castle, now and forever."

He traced the path of tears on one cheek and touched her lips. "That . . . that Lady Millie be healed, and her illness never return."

She accepted the bloom from Dermot, adding it to hers. She chose another sprig. "That Dr. McKendry know he has been a true friend to me during the most difficult time of my life."

He held up another. "That Lady Millie know how much I love her, that what I do and what I say comes from my heart."

The snow-colored flowers he handed to her danced in her vision. She couldn't look into Dermot's eyes. She feared the words she was about to say would never leave her lips if she were to admit how much she loved him, too.

"That when I am . . . " She took a deep breath, her face lifted to the sky. "That when I am gone, my dearest Dermot not suffer as he did before . . . when he lost the first love of his life."

Dermot had a largely unspoken rule that he lived by. Regardless of how close the acquaintance, one did not inquire into their past. Even with his partner, Wynne Melfort, whatever each man knew about the other's history, that knowledge had been offered, never solicited.

Millie knew about Susan, and she told him right away that she'd learned about his heartbreak the day they visited the museum. She assumed he'd be upset with Turner, but he wasn't. His old friend's concern was heartfelt; he'd stood by Dermot when he couldn't help himself. If ever he felt the need to explain his past to anyone, the time was now.

She clutched the bouquet of white heather as he helped her rise and asked her to walk with him.

"Susan and I were young," he began. "Our attraction was immediate and mutual. Both her parents were dead, but she came from an old landed family. She was the ward of her oldest brother, and he had no objection to our proposed engagement. When I think back on it now, it all happened so quickly."

Dermot knew so little about the workings of the human mind then, or about the diseases that afflicted people who pretended to be happy.

"She was beautiful, loving, kind. But at the same time, she was troubled. With each passing month of our engagement, I grew more worried about her. She would say or do things that would confuse me. Moments of anguish that she would deny having. Comments about the hopelessness of life. I found out there were times when she'd not leave her room for days. Even now, I don't know what was the cause of her melancholy."

"One day, I happened to see her in an apothecary's shop near the Surgeons' Hall. She was buying arsenic."

Dermot never forgot the incidents with Susan prior to that day. Wanting to jump off North Bridge. Stepping in front of the mail coach. There were many. He took a deep breath. It was so hard to talk about it.

"I was worried. And then I made the mistake of speaking to her brother about it."

Millie linked her arm in his and brushed her cheek against his shoulder.

"I don't know what he said to her. But that same afternoon, she climbed to the top of Nelson's Monument on Calton Hill and stepped off."

They came to a stop by the pool at the bottom of the waterfall. The trees and the cliffs of the ravine blocked the sunlight, and the air was cold, but Dermot barely noticed it. News of Susan's death reached him the same evening.

"At first, I felt anger. I blamed her brother. Then, in the days that followed, a numbness set in. I wasn't even aware of it. A dark abyss opened, and I unknowingly descended into it. I was overwhelmed with grief; I know that now. I blamed myself. Melancholy incapacitated me, shut down my mind to the point that I couldn't even care for myself. Those who knew me feared I might do the same thing that Susan had done, so they committed me to an asylum in the shadows of Edinburgh Castle."

Ever since then, he'd allowed people to think he worked in an asylum after completing his medical education.

"How long were you there?"

"Three months. The time I spent there in Livingston Yards was a horror." The methods were barbaric. The abuse was rampant. As his mind began to heal itself, he became more and more aware of how inhumane the conditions were.

"But you survived. And then you became a ship's surgeon."

"I needed to get away from Edinburgh, away from Susan's memory. I needed to forget what I'd been through."

"And the navy needed surgeons," she whispered.

He nodded. "I was fortunate. I secured a place on the ship commanded by Wynne Melfort. I found in him a friend for life. And when the wars against the French and the Americans were over, I knew I had to come back and start an asylum where patients were treated with compassion and a sense of decency."

He looked down at Millie's hand. She was still clutching the white heather. He recalled her last wish.

"My reaction to her death was because of guilt. I had betrayed her trust. Rather than helping her myself, I reached out to someone who was less than capable. In my own mind, my actions were responsible for pushing her off that tower."

"But you weren't responsible. He was her brother."

"I know that now. But her brother wasn't really responsible, either. He may have handled things badly with her, but in the end, her illness was her own." Dermot turned Millie in his arms until she was facing him. "Today, I recognize my mistakes. I've learned from them. I'd like to think I'm a better man because of them. But what matters to me at this moment is what *you* think of me, now that you know all of it."

She flattened one hand against his chest. In her other, she held the heather. It sat like a white cloud beneath their chins.

Her eyes were clear and untroubled, and her face shone. "You're my dear friend. You entertain me and buoy my spirits. You have medical expertise that I'll need and rely on during the trials ahead of me. I still have worry and fear in me, but because of you, I also have hope. You are the extraordinary man I've come to love."

"Millie." The flowers pressed between them as he gathered her tightly. "I love you."

"And if you are truly to take this uncertain journey with me, I hope you'll consider becoming my husband and my lover for—"

"Forever. For eternity," he finished, kissing her lips.

Chapter 11

The Pennington family arrived at Bellhorne in a caravan of carriages. However sedate the old castle had been in recent days, it was now alive with children and smiling faces.

Millie waited two days, since that was how long it took for her siblings and their spouses to meet the new addition and for the initial chaos and excitement to settle a little. Also, it was enough time for Dermot to be introduced and become comfortable with family members he hadn't met before. As Millie expected, her mother fell in love with him right away, and her father was keen to exchange stories with the man he'd already heard so much about from Jo.

People can cope with difficulties they know about. They can't cope with what they don't know.

Feeling lied to is often more painful than hearing a difficult truth.

Dermot's words stayed with her during the days as she looked for an opportunity to talk to them.

At night, she'd go to his room. She was the seducer. She wanted to feel this side of love. She'd wanted to experience their first moments of intimacy together before she bore the scars of surgery.

Fervent. Magnificent. Loving. Whatever Millie's expectations had been, they didn't compare to the radiant glow she felt by the end of that first night. The second night had been even better as the desire he aroused in her took them both to thrilling and unknown heights of passion. And before she left his room before dawn this morning, he reminded her again that she was not alone and never would be.

This weight you carry...your parents have already sensed it.

Speak to them. They should know what you're struggling with.

The morning room in Bellhorne was the brightest and most cheerful in the castle at this time of day. Tall windows opened out into the rose gardens, and the very air in the room carried a feeling of hope. Millie met with her parents there on Saturday morning.

"He's the one, isn't he?" the earl asked in his usual brusque tone as soon as the doors were closed. "Dr. McKendry."

"We approve of him." The countess put a hand on her husband's arm, encouraging patience as he started to say more.

Millie wasn't surprised they knew. It had to be obvious. And thanks to Phoebe's whispering, she guessed everyone knew. She stepped away from the windows and faced her parents. Her father's age was becoming more marked every year, with his snow-white hair and his pronounced limp. But he was still tall and commanding, and his mind was sharper than ever. Her mother was a vision of strength. Whatever ailments might trouble a woman of her advancing years, Millie had never heard her complain of any. She was a lioness who, with courage and vigor, looked after her husband and her family.

They could deal with the news of her illness, Millie told herself.

"He's the one. He'll ask your permission sometime today."

"Of course," Lord Aytoun growled. "He's a fine man. No question. And if he's the one you want, then we stand with you. As always."

"But you didn't ask us here to discuss an engagement, did you?" Her mother's voice was soft. "I picked up something to read when we stopped overnight in Edinburgh. It had this handbill inside. Is it yours?"

In her hand she held the advertisement for the ship sailing to America. Millie had left it in the pages of the Byron book.

"I thought I might go away, but no longer."

Her mother started to stand, but her husband kept her seated beside him.

"Tell us what's wrong, Millie," he prompted.

She started to speak but stopped, biting hard on her lip. It hurt her to cause them even a moment's worry. She wished Dermot were here with her now.

Be honest with them. Tell them exactly what you need from them.

"Look at me. I'm fine. I feel no pain. I have no outward symptoms of anything. I appear to be standing here in perfect health."

The words spilled from her lips, but she realized the longer she waited, the more concerned they were getting. It showed in her mother's eyes and in the clenched jaws of her father.

"But I need an operation to remove a tumor in my breast tissue. I saw a physician in Edinburgh on my own, but Dermot knows there are others more capable of helping me. Experts right in the city. The best anywhere. And I plan to see them."

Millie didn't want to take a breath. She stared at the portrait of Sarah on the wall, for she couldn't bring herself to look into their faces.

"I'm going to fight this. I need to fix what's wrong. There are dangers, of course, but I'll be strong and brave. And I'll survive." She pushed herself to continue. "Dermot will stay with me through it all. But I need you two to be strong, as well. To be there for me. To support me with your confidence and to guide me if I happen to miss a step. If I forget to keep looking forward."

Strong arms slipped around her. Her father's arms, followed by another pair. Warm whispers of love and encouragement breathed against her ear. Her mother's voice.

"We love you, Millie. We'll always be there for you."

Chapter 12

The Abbey
Western Aberdeen
The Scottish Highlands

Dearest Dermot,

A chair is a piece of furniture — designed long before the time of the pharaohs — for sitting. Kindly make a note of this information, since it is particularly relevant when the aforenamed furniture is located in *my* work room.

You may retrieve the pile of books, journals, paper and (apparently) associated miscellaneous paraphernalia at your leisure. The items are currently located in the pig sty where Little Dermot (who, as you know, is hardly *little* any longer) is no doubt perusing the material with great interest.

Dearest Millie,

Vile slander! I must proclaim my blamelessness in the strongest terms! One must recall that I was shockingly distracted. Allow me to clarify. After wandering unknowingly into a lovely young woman's office this morning, I was seduced! You read that correctly, m'lady . . . *seduced!* She was not to be either rebuffed or denied.

What else was a man to do with the armful of work materials he was carrying but to put them down on the nearest chair?

P.S. Is it possible the aforementioned young lady retained a pocket watch that may have dropped from my coat as it was being stripped from the body?
P.P.S. For all his qualities, I don't believe Little Dermot has ever learned to tell time.
P.P.P.S. Never mind, I just found the timepiece in my waistcoat pocket.

Dearest Dermot,

Since we are proclaiming innocence, I must declare that seduction was hardly my intention. Not at first. The elderberry stain on your shirt from breakfast was too much for my nature — which, as you know — is inclined to correct disorder and chaos wherever I find it.

P.S. I'm overjoyed that you have found your watch. That was an anniversary gift and needs to be *treasured*.

Dearest Millie,

Catastrophe! I need you! I just spilled my coffee on my trousers. The mess is indescribable!

Dearest Dermot,

Come at once!

P.S. Come at once!

The note was not dry on the paper before the door burst open and slammed shut behind him.

Millie met him in the middle of her work room, impatiently undoing the buttons of his trousers. Dermot's hands were all over her, and she laughed as he fumbled with her skirts. She pushed at his coat, and he tugged at her dress even as he was kicking off his shoes.

"We have a bedroom," he reminded her.

"It's midday. Everyone will know."

Losing his balance when she yanked his waistcoat open, he staggered back against her writing desk. He started to fall, and Millie reached out for him. He grabbed for her. The tearing sound of his shoulder seam stopped them only for an instant.

"Hurry," she exclaimed. "We don't have much time."

"I'm certain you're mistaken, my love. It's nowhere near time for —"

The two of them froze, hearing the knock on the door. Dermot let out a frustrated breath. Millie hushed him into silence.

"Just a moment," she called out.

A flurry of activity ensued. Buttons were refastened haphazardly. Dermot had only one arm in his waistcoat before Millie was driving his coat onto his other arm. As she tried to smooth her dress, he was crawling on his hands and knees under her table looking for one of his shoes. When she hissed at him to hurry, he reversed direction and banged his head before overturning a chair. On his feet again, they looked at each other and tried to stop laughing. Wonderful disaster.

A moment later, their clothes had been reasonably straightened. Trouser bulges had been subdued. Hair had been smoothed down as much as possible.

Tucking in an errant tendril of hair behind her ear, Millie took a breath and tried to look serious. She nodded at Dermot, and he opened the door.

Two small boys—five and seven years old—stood waiting in the corridor. The older lad was reasonably clean, but the younger was not.

"Mother, he's testing my patience today."

Though the younger one could dirty his clothes walking from the drawing room to the Great Hall, today he was filthier than usual. And from the smell, she knew exactly were he'd been.

"I was just making him comfortable," he argued.

"Who were you making comfortable, dear?"

"The pig," the older lad shouted, tugging at the rope in his hand.

Joining them a second later was a pig, the size of a small pony, grinning at her.

"He had Little Dermot in my bed."

"He has a cold," the younger one said, appealing to his father. "He couldn't sleep in the pens, could he?"

As the children continued to argue, Millie exchanged a look with Dermot. Their two sons.

"Whatever am I going to do with you?"

"Baths, to begin with," Dermot suggested.

"Can Little Dermot take a bath with us too?"

Millie smiled at the snort of disgust from her older son. She was the happiest woman in the Highlands.

Thank you for taking the time to read *Dearest Millie*. If you enjoyed it, please consider telling your friends or posting a short review. Word of mouth is an author's best friend...and much appreciated.

Author's Note

We hope you enjoyed reading *Dearest Millie*. As with all of our novels, we have tried to combine the real and the imagined in this story.

The idea for this novel came to us during the years we went through a life-changing illness. During that time, laughter and support from family and loved ones and friends became an integral part of the healing.

In writing *Dearest Millie,* we were reminded that when a person is afflicted with a serious medical condition like cancer, sharing that news is a difficult and deeply personal decision. The same goes for melancholia — or as we know it today, depression.

In 1812, the popular English novelist Frances Burney wrote a number of letters to her sister about her mastectomy. She survived the surgery and lived to the advanced age of eighty-eight.

The history of depression is that of an innately human experience. As a mood or emotion, the experience of being melancholy or depressed is at the very heart of being human. Robert Burton wrote in 1621, "Melancholy in this sense is the character of mortality."

Dearest Millie is part of the series of stories about the Pennington family. The parents' generation included several stand-alone novels and a series. In the Scottish Dream Trilogy, the Pennington Family series gets underway as three brothers struggle with the memory of Emma, an enigmatic young woman whose tragic and mysterious death at Baronsford Castle threatens to divide the family forever.

Borrowed Dreams— Millicent Wentworth (introduced in *The Promise*) , driven to undo the evil wrought by her dead husband, must find a way to save her estate and free the innocent people he enslaves. Her only hope is a marriage—in name only—to Lyon Pennington, the Earl of Aytoun, a man devastated by a tragic accident that killed his wife and left him gravely wounded. These two are the parents of Millie in *Dearest Millie*.

Captured Dreams— Pierce Pennington (the younger brother of Lyon, *Borrowed Dreams*) and Portia Edwards search for family in Boston and in Scotland.

Dreams of Destiny— David Pennington, the youngest Pennington brother, and Gwyneth Douglas solve the mystery of Emma's murder.

The Pennington Family series moves into the Regency Era and follows the romantic adventures of the next generation

Romancing the Scot — Hugh Pennington, the eldest son of Lyon and Millicent (*Borrowed Dreams*), a scarred war-hero, opens a crate delivered to his estate and finds a beautiful, half-dead woman with a priceless jewel sown into her dress.

It Happened in the Highlands — Jo Pennington, the adopted daughter of Lyon and Millicent (*Borrowed Dreams, Romancing the Scot*), and Captain Wynne Melfort search for her birth-parents at an ancient abbey-turned-asylum in the Highlands. Dermot McKendry is introduced in this novel. And his charm and character win many hearts.

Sweet Home Highland Christmas (RITA© Award Finalist) — Gregory Pennington meets his match when he is tasked with conveying Freya Sutherland and her five-year-old niece from the Highlands to Baronsford for the annual Christmas Ball.

Sleepless in Scotland — Phoebe Pennington, the fourth sibling in the Pennington family, and Captain Ian Bell fall in love even as they are haunted by the murder of his sister. Millie plays an important part in this novel as her sister's companion and confidante.

In addition, we mention Dr. Isabella Murray Drummond in this novella. She is the heroine of *Highland Crown*, the first novel in the new Royal Highlander series, in which three extraordinary women in the Highlands of Scotland find courage to defy the world at a tumultuous moment when a new Scottish identity will be forged or a political assassination will divide a nation forever.

As authors, we love feedback. We write our stories for you. We'd love to hear what you liked, what you loved, and even what you didn't like. We are constantly learning, so please help us write stories that you will cherish and recommend to your friends. Please sign up for news and updates at www.maymcgoldrick.com/contact-us and follow us on BookBub.

Finally, if you enjoyed reading *Dearest Millie*, please leave a review.

Peace and Health!
Nikoo and Jim (writing as May McGoldrick)

You can visit us on our website:
www.maymcgoldrick.com/

Excerpt of
Highland Crown

Abbotsford, the Scottish Borders
September 1832

Some say I'm a hero. Some call me a traitor.

My time grows short now. I feel nothing in my right side. My hand lies inert on the bedclothes. The apoplexy has robbed me of any useful employment. I tried, but I cannot hold a pen. Not that it matters. Those exertions are behind me now.

Some will say that I, Sir Walter Scott — author of *Waverley* and *Rob Roy* and *Red Gauntlet* — invented the new Scotland. That I was the unfailing champion of the noble traditions of the past. That I revealed the Scottish identity all now wear with tartan-emblazoned pride.

What they say is a lie.

My family has brought down my bed and propped me up before the open window of my dining room. In the meadow outside, the yellow of the rockrose, the scarlet of the campion flower, the pure white of the ox-eyed daisies nearly blind me with their reckless brilliance. The water scratches over the pebbled shore of the Tweed at the end of the field, but instead, I hear the haunting voices of hungry, homeless Highlanders, dying by the thousands.

How many have died as the ancient hills continue to be cleared of their tenant farmers in the name of progress? Pushed from their homes, driven to the sea, to the cold, hard streets of our cities, to lands far away . . . if they survive the journey. All to make way for a few more sheep. All in the quest of a few more shillings.

I did what I believed at the time was right for Scotland. I convinced myself I could not let my country descend into the lawless chaos of bloody revolution, the throat of civility ripped out by the mob. It happened in France. The guillotine's dread machinery flew out of control, splashing far too much innocent blood into the streets in its ravaging thirst for the guilty. And the cobbled lanes of Paris were not yet dry when a new terror arose in the form of their arrogant tyrant Napoleon. I told myself I could not let that happen here. Not here. Not in my homeland.

But now I see the truth clearly, and the bitter gall of that knowledge rises into my throat. I spent a lifetime creating an image of Scotland I knew was not real. I closed my eyes to the suffering and the deaths of my own people, and instead told stories depicting the grandeur of an imagined Highland past. And as I worked, I held my tongue about the bloody decimation of the clans and their way of life. Men I dined with daily were profiting from the killing, and I said nothing. Worse, I, too, made money from it with my romantic tales.

Many are those who see me clearly. To them, I am Walter Scott—turncoat, bootlicking lackey of the British Crown. They say I sold the independence of Scotland for a shabby box of tawdry and meaningless honors. They say that because of me, the Scottish people will never be free again. That I betrayed them for a wee bit of fleeting fame and the price of a few books.

Now, after all these years, I find myself forced to agree. And that is all the more difficult to bear because I lie here with Death stalking the shadows of Abbotsford.

He's been dogging my faltering steps for some time now.

This fever struck me as we returned from our travels. Rome and Naples, Florence and Venice. Those places had offered no relief. Death was coming for me. London was covered in yellow fog when we arrived, but the rest is a blur. They tell me I lay close to dying for weeks. I don't recall. Then the final journey home. The steady rumbling rhythm of a steamboat remains in my mind, but I remember very little of that. I only know that I am home now.

Two of my hunters have been turned out into the meadow. Fine mounts. The golden sun glistens on their powerful shoulders as they begin to graze. I wish I could be as content, but life has buffeted me about, and the choices I've made give me no respite. Nor should they.

My mind returns again and again to the upheaval of 1820, to the "Rising."

We called those men and women radicals, when all they wanted were the rights and freedoms of citizens. In the name of equality and fraternity, they cried out for representation. They demanded the vote. Some called for an end to what they saw as the iron fist of Crown rule. They wanted to sever our northern kingdom from England and restore the ancient parliament of Scotland. In my lifetime, those men and women were the last chance for Scotland's independence, and I blinded myself to their cause. And when Westminster made it treason to assemble and protest, they willingly gave their lives. The heroic blood of the Bruce and the Wallace ran in their veins. I see that now. Too late.

That same year, that same month, as the blood flowed, I returned to Scotland from

Westminster bearing my new title. Even now, I feel the weight of the king's sword on my shoulders. But as I reveled proudly in my accomplishments, the cities across the land were tinderboxes, threatening to explode in a wild conflagration of civil war. The weavers and the other tradesmen in Glasgow and Edinburgh had just brought the country's affairs to a halt with their strikes. Some of the reformers had courageously marched on the ironworks at Carron to seize weapons.

Scotland teetered on the brink of anarchy. I was afraid. So I took the well-worn path of weak men.

My single moment of courage came when I saved a woman who would help change the course of history.

Isabella Murray Drummond. A marvel of this modern age. A doctor, no less, who'd studied at the university in Wurzburg, where her eminent father held a professor's chair. When he passed away, she married an Edinburgh physician who'd gone to further his studies under the tutelage of her father. He was a widower with a growing daughter. She was a single woman left with a younger sister and a small inheritance. It was a marriage of convenience.

Isabella, who had the loveliness of Venus and the bearing of a queen, saved me from losing my leg—lame since my childhood—after the carriage accident in Cowgate. I was carried to their infirmary. The husband was away, but I was fortunate that she was there, for Isabella was the very angel of mercy I needed at that moment, and her skill as a physician saved my life.

No matter my regrets, or what I do to right wrongs, or what I write to change the fate of Scotland, some will always think me a traitor. I know now that I have helped in giving away my country's chance for independence . . . perhaps forever . . . in return for a peace that was profitable for a few. But one thing in my life that I'll never regret was my action on that woman's behalf when the time came.

The news spread across the city. Isabella Drummond's husband was dead, and she was in hiding with her sister and her stepdaughter. The government had declared her an enemy of the Crown, placed a bounty upon her head. Her husband's rebellious allies wanted her, as well, believing she'd inform on them.

I succeeded in helping the women escape from the city, far to the north where they would board a ship bound for Canada. She was to join all those Highlanders who were journeying to a new life. But she would never board any ship. She would never reach the shores of that far-off place.

For on the rugged coast of the Highlands, she disappeared . . . and lived a truer adventure than ever flowed from my pen.

About the Author

USA Today Bestselling Authors Nikoo and Jim have crafted over forty fast-paced, conflict-filled historical and contemporary novels and two works of nonfiction under the pseudonyms May McGoldrick and Jan Coffey.

These popular and prolific authors write historical romance, suspense, mystery, and young adult novels. They are four-time Rita Finalists and the winners of numerous awards for their writing, including the *Romantic Times Magazine* Reviewers' Choice Award, the Daphne DeMaurier Award, three NJRW Golden Leaf Awards, two Holt Medallions, and the Connecticut Press Club Award for Best Fiction. Their work is included in the Popular Culture Library collection of the National Museum of Scotland.

Printed in Great Britain
by Amazon

11336097R00079